Trisha remained on the sofa, feeling numb. She kept remembering the conversations she'd had with Tucker about the accident. He had asked her questions. What had she told him? Had he been trying to find out what she remembered in order to vent and grieve? Or did he have a deeper motive? One that included protecting himself?

She shook her head, unable and unwilling to dwell on that idea. Tucker had loved Christina. If he was one bit responsible for her death, he'd admit it . . . wouldn't he? If only she could remember more details. *If only.*

Telling Christina Goodbye

Lurlene McDaniel

Telling Christina Goodbye

BANTAM BOOKS

NEW YORK • TORONTO • LONDON • SYDNEY • AUCKLAND

RL: 5.3, AGES 12 AND UP

TELLING CHRISTINA GOODBYE

A Bantam Book / April 2002

Text copyright © 2002 by Lurlene McDaniel

Cover art copyright © 2002 by David Loew

ISBN: 0-553-57087-0

**Visit us on the Web! www.randomhouse.com/teens
Educators and librarians, for a variety of teaching tools, visit us at
www.randomhouse.com/teachers**

Published simultaneously in the United States and Canada

Bantam Books is an imprint of Random House Children's Books, a
division of Random House, Inc. BANTAM BOOKS and the rooster
colophon are registered trademarks of Random House, Inc. Bantam
Books, 1540 Broadway, New York, New York 10036.

PRINTED IN THE UNITED STATES OF AMERICA

OPM 10 9 8 7 6 5 4

This book is dedicated to Nathan, Megan, and Andy . . . who lived it.

February 12, 1995

"FOR I KNOW THE PLANS I HAVE FOR YOU," DECLARES
THE LORD, "PLANS TO PROSPER YOU AND NOT TO HARM
YOU, PLANS TO GIVE YOU HOPE AND A FUTURE."

JEREMIAH 29:11
(NEW INTERNATIONAL VERSION)

Telling Christina Goodbye

One

❧

During the first week of classes after Christmas break, between fourth and fifth periods at Mooresville High School, Trisha Thompson went looking for Christina Eckloe. She found her best friend crying in the girls' bathroom. Her sobs were muffled and sounded almost like a kitten mewing, hardly the reflection of a breaking heart, but Trisha wasn't fooled. She'd heard Christina cry before. And it didn't take a rocket scientist to figure out why. Tucker Hanson.

Trisha slipped into the unlocked stall where Christina was hiding, her hands covering her face. Trisha unrolled a swath of toilet paper and handed it to her friend. "Here, use this. It's more absorbent than your palms."

Christina took the wad of paper without looking up. She wiped her eyes and blew her nose. "H-how did you find me?"

"When you didn't show up for lunch, I started checking the bathrooms. This was my third stop."

"Wh-where are the others? I don't want them to see me like this."

"Kim and Darby went on to class. Cody's waiting outside in the hall."

"Why couldn't I get a guy like Cody?" Christina asked.

"You mean instead of a jerk like Tucker? That's always been my question to you, hasn't it?" Trisha felt angry. "Tucker *is* the reason you're crying, isn't he? I mean, he usually is the reason you cry."

Christina nodded.

Trisha sighed. "What'd he do this time?"

"We had a fight."

"Over what?"

"You don't have to talk to me like I'm a child," Christina said. She stood shakily and edged past Trisha out of the stall.

Trisha followed. "Sorry. But you've been

fighting with Tucker off and on for years. It gets to me because he's not nice to you."

Christina bent over a sink and splashed cold water on her face. "You just don't understand."

"Enlighten me."

"This time it really was my fault," Christina said. "I ran into Bill Lawler at the library last night. Tucker was supposed to pick me up at nine, but we'd had a fight that afternoon and he didn't show."

Trisha rolled her eyes.

"Anyway," Christina continued while drying her face on a paper towel, "Bill offered to drive me home and on the way we stopped off and had coffee. Someone must have seen us together and told Tucker, because when he picked me up for school this morning he was really upset. I tried to explain that there's nothing between me and Bill, but he won't believe me."

"So now he's mad because you had coffee with Bill? What's wrong with that?"

"I'm Tucker's girl. I shouldn't have gone out with another guy."

"Oh, please!" Trisha crossed her arms. "You didn't go out on a date, you had a coffee together. How can he be that insecure? You've been with him since eighth grade."

The entire class knew about Tucker and Christina's relationship. He had been voted Mr. Most Popular and this year's Homecoming King; she had been selected as Miss Best Personality and Homecoming Queen. Kids saw them as perfect for each other, beautiful people who had been going together forever and who were destined to always be a couple. Only Trisha and her boyfriend, Cody McGuire, knew about the tumultuous nature of the pairing. To Trisha's way of thinking, Tucker was often hateful to Christina, sarcastic and even rude. Trisha didn't understand why they stayed together. Christina could have any guy she wanted at Mooresville.

"Are you saying Cody wouldn't object if you were seen in public having coffee with some other guy by people who think you've got an exclusive relationship with him?" Christina sounded defensive.

"Frank Russo and I go out all the time and Cody doesn't feel threatened."

"You're coeditors of the yearbook. Of course you go out all the time. Plus Frank has Abby Harrison for a girlfriend."

Trisha ignored Christina's logic. "The point

is, Cody *trusts* me. After all the years you've been with Tucker, he should trust you too."

Christina looked dejected. "That's what I told him, but he's still angry."

"Then that's his problem, not yours. He needs to get over it, cut you some slack."

"There are other things too." Christina fished in her purse for lip gloss. "I've been accepted at the University of Vermont—"

"But that's wonderful," Trisha interrupted.

Christina smiled for the first time. "Mom and Dad think so too, especially since it came with a ten-thousand-dollar scholarship."

Trisha was speechless. She'd always known Christina was smart, but this really proved it.

"It's Dad's alma mater, so he really wants me to go there," Christina added.

"So why wouldn't you?"

"Tucker hates the idea. He can't accept that I would go so far from Indiana, or him. He's really bummed out about it. He wants me to go someplace in-state, like IU."

Indiana University at Indianapolis was a good hundred and fifty miles from Mooresville, a midsized town in the middle of nowhere. Trisha had moved to Mooresville with her

parents and kid brother five years before when
her father, an insurance agent, had taken over
the job of area manager for his company. To
Trisha, after having lived in a sprawling suburb
of Chicago all her life, Mooresville had seemed
like the most boring place on earth. When
Christina had befriended her in seventh grade,
that had made all the difference. Then, when
they'd both started at the high school, Trisha
met Cody, and having him for a boyfriend for
two years had turned Mooresville into the center of the universe.

"How can Tucker expect you to change your
plans—your future—for him? Why doesn't he
change his plans for you?" Trisha asked.

Christina shook her head. "He has to start at
the community college because his grades are
poor—if he decides to go to college at all. I
know you and Cody are planning to go to IU
together, so don't pretend you're making any
sacrifice for each other in that respect."

"Point taken," Trisha said. "We do plan on
going off to IU together, but first we both have
to be accepted." She and Cody had applied,
but acceptance letters wouldn't be sent out
until early spring. "But I'm telling you, if I had

a valid scholarship offer, I'd take it. Tucker should be happy for you."

Trisha stared at Christina's reflection and her own while Christina put on powder. Christina was blond, with a pretty heart-shaped face and clear blue eyes. Trisha's plain dark hair—which she was letting grow long and which now was lank and scraggly—and brown eyes looked drab next to her friend. But Christina wasn't conceited about her looks; she was genuinely congenial and friendly. People liked Christina because Christina liked people.

"We've missed fifth period," Christina said with a sigh. "You shouldn't have skipped on my account. I don't want you to get into trouble."

Trisha shrugged. "I skipped world lit, big deal. I've read the chapter already, and you know Mr. Childess can put a dead person to sleep."

Christina raked a comb through her hair. "You're the one I'm going to miss the most if I go away to Vermont, not Tucker."

Trisha put her hand on Christina's arm before they stepped into the hall. "Don't let Tucker make you do something you don't want to do. If he really loves you, he'll give you some room to do what you want, go where you want."

"You sound like my mother."

"Hey, no need to insult me."

They both laughed. Trisha *had* offered a standard refrain, one worthy of any adult. The truth was, she knew she was right. Tucker Hanson was trouble. He always had been and he always would be. How could Christina be so blind that she couldn't see that?

"Ah, Tuck's not so bad," Cody said as he shut his locker in the crowded halls after school.

While they'd walked from her locker to his, Trisha had told him about her conversation in the bathroom with Christina. "He tries to control her, and she won't stand up to him," Trisha grumbled now, not pleased with Cody's assessment of Tucker. "I think that's pretty bad."

Cody grinned down at her. "Like how you tell me to meet you at the library at seven and don't be late or else?"

"That's different and you know it. I'm talking about the way he blows up if she goes against his wishes. The very idea of telling her where to go to college. Or who she can have coffee with. You don't treat me like that."

"So he's a little jealous. We guys get that way when somebody makes a move on our girl."

"A move! We're talking Billy Lawler here. The guy's no more a threat to Tucker than I am to Miss America."

Cody put his arm around Trisha's shoulders. "I'm sure Lawler thought he'd died and gone to heaven when the lovely Christina graced him with her presence, so you're right—Tuck has no reason to worry. But it's just his way."

"Don't defend him." Trisha pulled on her gloves before they walked out into the snow-covered parking lot.

Cody jammed his hand into her coat pocket and pulled her closer. "They've been acting that way for years. I can't see it changing."

"But why? Christina's smart. Why does she let him treat her like she's stupid?"

"They love each other," Cody said with a shrug. "Just like I love you." He nuzzled her neck as they walked to his car.

"But you treat me right. That's the difference."

"I do, do I? I can change that." He took the lapels of her coat in both hands and pulled her against his chest. His eyes danced mischievously. "Into the car, girl," he growled.

She arched one eyebrow. "You going to make me?"

"I'm bigger than you. And uglier, so watch your step."

"Don't make me wrestle you and humiliate you in front of the school," she said, pulling herself up to her full height of five feet, three inches.

He kissed the tip of her nose. "Wrestle me. Please."

A horn honked two rows over and a male voice shouted, "I said, get in the car right now!"

Startled, Trisha and Cody looked over to see Tucker driving beside a walking Christina, who was pointedly ignoring him.

Tucker called Christina some names and demanded she do what he said. Christina stopped, and so did Tucker's car.

"You want a ride, Chrissy?" Trisha yelled. "Cody and I can take you home."

"Sure," Cody said. "Come on."

"I'm taking her home," Tucker said. "We have to talk, don't we, honey?"

Christina turned toward them, and Trisha saw the tracks of tears on her cheeks. *"Don't get in the car,"* Trisha said under her breath. *"Don't go with him."*

"Thanks," Christina said to Trisha and Cody after an agonizing minute. "But I'll go with Tucker. It's all right."

Christina opened the car door, and Trisha's heart sank. "I'll call you just as soon as I get home," she called out as Tucker gunned the engine.

Christina hadn't even gotten the door shut before Tucker sped out of the parking lot, tires spinning on the slick, blackened snow. "Jerk," Trisha said, watching him turn the corner without even stopping at the Yield sign.

Cody slipped his arm around her again. "Let's go."

Tears filled Trisha's eyes. "She didn't have to go with him, you know."

"I know." Cody opened his car door and helped Trisha inside. "I'll talk to him, okay? Maybe he'll listen. He's not really a bad guy." He got in, turned over the engine, and turned up the heater. "He's scared of losing her. If she goes away, he's afraid she won't come back."

"I hope she doesn't," Trisha said, drying her eyes and simmering with anger. "I hope she leaves him flat."

Two

❦

Trisha banged into her house and was part-way up the stairs to her room when her mother intercepted her. "Slow down. I need you to do me a favor."

"I have to call Chrissy."

"Wasn't she at school today?"

"Yes, but—"

"Then it will keep. Charlie has to be at bas-ketball practice in fifteen minutes, and you have to take him."

"Aw, Mom . . . hanging around the gym for an hour waiting for him to finish practice is the pits."

Her mother gave her a level look. "You don't

say? This from the girl who swore that she'd be my virtual slave if I allowed her to get her license last October."

"Yes, but—"

"No buts. Do it."

Just then, twelve-year-old Charlie came around the corner from the kitchen, bouncing his basketball and eating an apple.

"Kill the ball," their mother said.

Charlie grabbed the ball in mid-dribble. "She taking me? She drives like an old lady. I'll be late and Coach makes us do laps if we're late."

"So hitchhike," Trisha snapped.

"Stop arguing," their mother said. "Just go."

"If Chrissy calls—"

"I'll tell her you'll call her back," her mother said.

Trisha marched out the front door, trailing Charlie and grumbling all the way.

The gym smelled like sweaty socks, and the noise level was giving Trisha a headache. She sat in the upper bleachers trying to concentrate on an assignment and ignore the drill work of her kid brother's team below. It was a losing battle.

"How're you doing?"

Startled, Trisha looked up and saw Tucker standing on the bleacher two rows above her. "Can I join you?"

She had forgotten that his brother, Jeremy, played on the same middle school team as Charlie. "It's a free country," she told him.

"Where's Cody?" Tucker asked, sitting on the bench above hers.

"At his job at the new Home Depot."

"I forgot he kept working after Christmas break."

"He says the money's good and since football season's over, he's got the extra time." She fidgeted because she didn't have much to say to Tucker. "How's Chrissy?" she finally asked.

"Mad at me."

"Go figure."

Tucker smiled sheepishly. "All right . . . so I lost my cool today."

Trisha didn't say anything.

"You don't like me very much, do you?"

No, she thought, but said, "Maybe I just don't like the way you treat Chrissy."

Tucker leaned back on his elbows, studying her. "I really love her, you know. Tell her that for me."

"Why should I?"

"Because she listens to you."

"Not really." Trisha knew that if Christina really listened to her, she'd dump Tucker.

"Would you also tell her not to go off to Vermont?" He sounded solicitous, as if he really wanted the favor.

"It's a great opportunity, Tucker. The scholarship is awesome."

"If she stays, we can be together," he said as if she hadn't spoken. "I don't want her to go."

"It's a long time until September. She deserves her chance. Maybe you'll change your mind."

"No. She's all I ever wanted."

Trisha knew there were kids who'd think Tucker's statement was romantic. She did not. She thought he just wanted to have his way. "Then treat her like it," she suggested. "Yelling at her, telling her how to act and who she can see isn't winning her over, you know?"

For a moment, a dark glower crossed his face. The look passed, and he stood. "You girlfriends really stick together, don't you? I'm the best thing that ever happened to Chrissy. She'll never find a guy who cares about her the way I do."

He started down the bleachers toward the floor, clattering all the way and making everybody else in the gym glance over. Trisha watched, silently fuming over his arrogance. They were certainly worlds apart when it came to the definition of love. She thought of love as a gift one person gave freely to another. Tucker Hanson figured it was something a person used like a rope to tie another down. And worse, it made Trisha want to scream that he had captured the heart of Christina, her best friend.

On Saturday, Christina talked Trisha into going with her to the county nursing home where she was a volunteer. Trisha wasn't crazy about the place—some of the elderly people looked so frail that it broke her heart, but Christina always said, "It makes me feel like I'm doing something useful. And it makes me feel like Grandpa's watching from heaven and happy about me helping others." Christina's grandfather had lived with her family until it had become too difficult to care for him. They'd transferred him to an assisted living facility, where he'd died two years before.

As they walked inside the old building, Christina said, "Thanks a bunch, Trisha. The staff is shorthanded because of the flu bug."

"What are friends for?" Trisha said, dismayed by the very atmosphere of the place. The air smelled of disinfectant and medicine. The floors were clean but carpetless, the walls an institutional shade of pale green. Trisha stepped around an old lady in a wheelchair. The woman was asleep, tied to the chair so that she wouldn't fall out. Trisha and Christina checked in at the front desk, then again at the nurses' station.

"You're a sight for sore eyes," said Mrs. Kimble, the head floor nurse.

"You remember my friend Trisha. She's helping out today."

Mrs. Kimble's big smile lit her coffee-colored face. "Good to see you. And nice of you to lend a hand." She picked up a chart. "Chrissy, can you feed Mr. Tappin in room six? He just can't go down to the cafeteria anymore." Mrs. Kimble looked at Trisha. "Can I get you to take the patients on this list down to the exercise room? They're all in wheelchairs, but they can't take themselves."

Trisha gathered the eight patients on the list one by one and wheeled them into the exercise room, where a cheerful aerobics instructor led them in stretching exercises and coordination drills. Some could barely lift their arms. Trisha helped one woman grip a one-pound barbell and curl it to her chest. The woman offered a wide toothless grin when she succeeded in doing one curl all on her own.

After the exercise class, Trisha folded and stacked towels and linen in the laundry room. It was after five when she wheeled the last of her charges into the main cafeteria for supper and went looking for Christina. "She's with Mr. Tappin," Mrs. Kimble said when Trisha asked about her friend. "Honestly, that old man won't do anything for anybody except her. Why, I've seen him shove his tray on the floor if he doesn't like the person who comes in to feed him. He won't feed himself. Why, he'd starve to death if we didn't poke food in his mouth three times a day." She shook her head, muttering to herself. "Alzheimer's is a mean condition. Yes, it surely is."

Trisha went to Mr. Tappin's room and stopped at the doorway. Christina was on her knees in front of the old man's wheelchair, patiently feeding him spoonfuls of mashed potatoes. Trisha heard Christina saying, "Now open up wide. This stuff is so yummy. And if you finish all your supper, I'll read you a story."

The old man stared straight ahead but opened his mouth. Although he closed his lips over the spoon, the potatoes oozed out of the sides of his mouth and dribbled down his chin. Christina dabbed his chin with a napkin and offered another spoonful. Trisha watched, mesmerized. Christina never ran out of patience, and the old man opened his mouth obediently whenever she asked. Mrs. Kimble was right: Christina had a gift for working with the old man.

After they left the nursing home, the girls stopped for burgers before going home. "I don't know how you do it," Trisha said, nibbling on fries. "That place makes me sad."

Christina smiled and shrugged. "I like to help. I've sometimes thought about going into nursing."

"You'd be good at it."

"Vermont has a nursing program," Christina added. "Mrs. Kimble says that some of the smaller hospitals are letting surgical nurses help with routine surgeries. That means lending a hand to the surgeon, maybe even closing a patient."

"You mean like sewing somebody up?" Trisha made a face. She didn't find anything appealing about blood and wounds.

Christina laughed. "Somebody has to do it. Why not me?"

"If that's what you really want to do, you should do it." Trisha sipped her cola. "Does this mean you're taking the Vermont scholarship?"

Christina's smile faded. "I'm still not sure about that yet."

Trisha told her about the conversation she'd had with Tucker days before. "He wants me to talk you out of going, but I won't do it. If anything, I'm telling you to go."

Christina looked resigned. "He's been putting pressure on me for sure. He makes me feel like I'll be deserting him. He doesn't see it as a possible future for both of us."

"Why do you put up with it? With him? You don't have to."

"I've known Tucker for more than half my life. He's just always been there for me."

"You want loyalty? Get a dog. Tucker's immature and manipulative."

Christina dipped her head; her blond hair fell forward, covering her face. "Don't say mean things about him, please. He loves me and he doesn't mean to hurt me."

"But you're not happy. Maybe the perfect guy is out there—maybe in Vermont—who'll love you and treat you right."

"I think about that too." Christina raised her head. Her blue eyes looked serious. "When Tucker's sweet to me, when he's kind, he makes me feel better than any other person in the world. I can't imagine a day going by and not seeing him or talking to him. He knows what I'm thinking, he knows what I'm feeling, sometimes just by looking at me. It's hard to explain."

Trisha thought Christina's explanation sounded creepy, but didn't tell her so. At a nearby table, a group of guys horsed around, blowing the paper casings off their straws and slapping the table surface with flattened palms. *They're flirting*, she thought. And why not? They'd caught sight of Christina.

"You make him sound like Santa Claus,"

Trisha said with a sigh. " 'He knows when you've been bad or good. . . .' "

This made Christina laugh. "You can turn the most serious moments into jokes, Trisha. How do you do it?"

"It's a gift. So what do you want me to tell you? Stay with Tucker and spend the rest of your life on his roller coaster? Go to Vermont and see how you feel about him after he's not in your face every waking minute? Both are options."

"You're lucky. You see things in black and white. I don't. But I am working on it. I just need time to sort through it all. All right?"

"What do you want me to do?"

"Just be my friend. Don't take so many pot-shots at Tucker. It only hurts my feelings."

Trisha sighed. That was the difference between them—she was a take-no-prisoners kind of person and Christina had a heart the size of Texas. "One more thing, then I promise to shut up about it," she said. "Don't let who you're with define who you are. Sorry if that sounds corny, but it's what I think."

"Is that your absolute final word on the matter?"

"Well, maybe for tonight." Trisha grinned. "Now, turn around and smile at those guys at the table over there before they break their necks trying to get your attention. It's the humanitarian thing to do, you know."

Three

On Thursday, a blizzard blew across northern Indiana, shutting down school for two days. Trisha was going stir-crazy when Cody surprised her, arriving on skis the afternoon the snow-plows were digging out the town and rural roads. "Ski patrol!" he shouted from her front porch.

She squealed, yanked open the front door, and threw her arms around him. "I can't believe this! Come in! I'll fix hot chocolate. How long did it take you to get here?"

He released his skis and propped them on the porch. "About thirty minutes across the fields. The snow must be three feet deep. And some hot chocolate would be great."

She took him downstairs to the family room, where she'd already established a comfort zone with pillows and blankets in front of a cozy fire, and a stack of videos. "If I have to watch *The Matrix* one more time, I'll go crazy," she said. They'd only lost power for an hour on the first day of the storm. Now there was nothing to do but wait until crews cleared the roads.

"But it's such a cool movie," Charlie piped up.

"Get lost," Trisha told him.

"No way."

She pointed to the stairs. "Hike, buster."

"I'll tell Mom."

Their parents were upstairs in the kitchen doing some kind of project. "She'll back me. Cody's gone to extreme effort to be with me, not you."

"There's nothing to do up there!"

"You have ten games for your PlayStation. I got you one for Christmas—"

"Hold it." Cody stepped between Trisha and Charlie. "Tell you what, sport. Give Trisha and me some time together, and I'll come up and play a round of Spider-Man with you."

Charlie considered the offer. "Just an hour?"

Trisha rolled her eyes. "Blackmailer."

"One hour." Cody set the alarm on his watch.

"You two going to get all kissy-kissy?" Charlie made a face like a fish puckering its lips.

"Hit the road," Trisha said, picking up a pillow to throw at her kid brother.

"One hour!" Charlie bounded up the stairs, making sucking sounds.

"He's such a brat," Trisha said, flopping onto a row of pillows.

"Well, he's right about one thing. I am going to kiss you." Cody swept her into his arms.

His kiss was long and deep and Trisha felt her knees go weak. He pulled back and touched her cheek tenderly. "That was worth braving the cold for."

"Thank you for rescuing me," she said, laying her cheek against his chest. His wool sweater felt scratchy and smelled of cinnamon.

"Now about that hot chocolate . . ."

She went upstairs and into the kitchen, where her father had a dismantled garbage disposal spread over the kitchen table. Her mother stirred a large pot of soup on the stove. "Cody's here," Trisha said.

"You don't say," her mother said. "And in all this snow too. How gallant."

"Ah, love," her father said. "Ain't it beautiful?"

Trisha ignored their teasing and poured milk and cocoa mix into a mug and put it into the microwave. "Can he stay for supper?"

"Of course."

"The roads should be clear enough for me to drive him home tonight," her father said.

Trisha had half hoped that her parents would let Cody sleep on the sofa downstairs. He had once before, and she had sneaked down in the middle of the night and snuggled in his arms until dawn. Nothing had happened between them, but it had felt really good to be held, to hear him breathing softly in her ear. Her parents would have killed her if they'd known. The microwave beeped and she carried the cup down to the basement, where Cody was flipping through a stack of CDs.

They plopped on the sofa and Cody drained the chocolate in about two gulps. "Thirsty?" she asked.

He grinned. "It was a long trek."

"I'm glad you came."

"I couldn't help myself. I kept seeing you with my arms around you."

She felt like melting. "You thought about being with me for two days straight?"

"That and your mother's cooking," he added, nuzzling her ear.

She pinched him hard, and next thing they were wrestling and laughing. When the alarm on his watch sounded, she was disappointed. She didn't want to give him up to Charlie.

"Duty calls," Cody said, turning off the alarm.

"Hey, Cody! Time's up!" Charlie called from the top of the stairs.

"This from a kid who can't remember which entrance of the school to wait in front of when I go to pick him up," Trisha grumbled.

Cody kissed her. "Be back in a bit."

Trisha sighed, immediately bored. She picked up the phone and called Christina. "Guess what?" she said when her friend answered. Trisha told her about Cody's arrival on skis.

"Lucky you. I'm stuck here with my parents. And all Dad does is pressure me to accept the Vermont offer, while Tucker's begging me to stay around."

"But you *have* to go to college," Trisha said.

"Oh, I'll go, but maybe not so far away. Honestly, I think my parents want to get rid of me."

"No way. They just don't want you to pass up a golden opportunity."

"Whose side are you on, anyway?"

"Yours," Trisha said, meaning it with all her heart. "When do you have to decide for sure?"

"By the end of February."

"That's next month."

"Tell me about it."

They hung up, and when Cody finally returned from his game with Charlie, Trisha told him about the conversation. "Tucker's being really selfish," she said. "Did you ever say anything to him?"

"A little." He didn't meet her eyes.

"What? You're not telling me everything."

"He wants to double next Friday night. Thought it would be fun if we went to the Henderson game with him and Chrissy."

Henderson was a town thirty miles away and its high school was one of Mooresville's chief athletic rivals. The Mooresville basketball team, the Fighting Scots, had won seven of their last ten matches. This time, the game was on Henderson's court.

"I like Chrissy and I love you," Trisha said. "Do we have to take Tucker with us?"

Cody laughed. "It was his idea, remember?"

She made a face. "It's all right with me. Maybe our presence will help Tucker stay off Chrissy's case."

"Tuck will drive. I'll come here and they can pick us up together."

"You know he almost started a riot at the Chesterton game."

"That was last year. I'm sure he's going to behave himself at this one."

She laced her fingers through Cody's. The air between them felt charged, like electricity without an outlet. Her internal radar went off. Something wasn't right. "Are you sure you're telling me everything?"

"Why wouldn't I?"

"You found another girl you want to date and you want to break up with me." She blurted out her deepest fear, not believing it, but using it to make him open up.

"No way." He gave her a disgusted look. "I don't want to ever break up with you."

"Okay, it was a reach, but I know there's something you're not telling me."

"Do I look that guilty?"

"You look like you want to tell me something but don't know how."

He looked sheepish. "I never could fool you."

"Why would you want to?"

"Because I told Tucker I wouldn't say anything. He made me promise."

"But you want to tell me, don't you?"

"You're not going to like it."

"Is it about him and Christina?"

Cody nodded. "I wish Tuck had never told me. It's like carrying around a ticking time bomb."

By now, curiosity was eating Trisha alive. "I can keep a secret," she told him.

"Better than me, I hope."

"I won't say anything."

"You can't tell Chrissy." Cody's expression was serious, challenging.

Trisha nibbled on her bottom lip, hesitant to make a promise she might regret. "Is it something bad?"

"Not really. It's supposed to be a good thing. I—um—I'm just not sure it is in this case."

"Well, now you've got to tell me because if you don't, I'll burst, and how will that look to all our friends? Me smeared all over the halls. And on your new sweater too!"

He grinned, leaned forward, and kissed her. "I can't have that happening now, can I? What a mess."

She waited, sitting on the edge of the sofa, watching his face as he struggled with an internal war—to tell her, or to keep his promise to Tucker. Finally, Cody turned and took a deep breath. "Tucker's giving Chrissy a ring for Valentine's Day. He plans to ask her to marry him—just as soon as they graduate in June."

Four

There's more than one way to win a war. Trisha was aware of that truth every day she carried around the secret that Cody had shared with her. Tucker was going to sidestep the competition and go straight for the win: ask Christina to marry him and keep her from going off to Vermont forever. And worse, Trisha wasn't sure Christina would have the gumption to refuse his proposal.

Valentine's Day was less than two weeks away, and Trisha guiltily harbored her knowledge. She couldn't let Cody down by telling Christina. And she couldn't let on to Tucker that she knew. Her only hope was to try to talk Christina out of accepting the ring when her friend told her about the proposal, as Trisha knew Christina would. Until then, Trisha forced herself to keep her mouth shut.

Afraid that she might let something slip, she was glad that the yearbook kept her busy after school so she didn't have to spend more time with Christina. The task was made even harder when Christina came up to her with a radiant smile and said, "Tucker is treating me like a queen these days."

"Doesn't that make you suspicious?"

"Why should it? He's helping me remember all the reasons why I loved him in the first place."

"So, no more pressure to make you give up your scholarship?"

"He told me to make up my own mind about it." Christina looked puzzled. "You don't look like you're happy for me."

"I'm happy," Trisha said quickly. "I was only wondering why he backed off."

"Because he loves me, silly. And he wants me to do what I want."

Trisha had to turn away for fear that Christina would see how angry she was about Tucker's newfound attitude. *The pressure's just about to begin*, she wanted to tell her friend. But she couldn't.

On the night of the Henderson game, Trisha and Cody piled in the backseat of Tucker's car. "There's a blanket on the floor," Tucker said. "My heater's not working all that great. But I didn't think the two of you'd mind covering up with a blanket. And no one in the front seat's going to be looking back there doing a hand check, if you know what I mean."

Trisha didn't like his insinuation. Cody tucked the blanket around them. "We'll behave," he said.

Christina offered Trisha a candy bar. "Want some? It's dinner for me. I got tied up at the nursing home. Couldn't get Mr. Tappin to eat tonight."

"That old fart?" Tucker said. "Why do you waste your time?"

"Don't call him names," Christina said. "He's a pitiful old man who needs extra help. You know, he's been there three years and he's never once had a visitor."

"Whatever," Tucker said with a wave of his hand. "I'll buy you a hot dog at the game."

Trisha felt sorry for Mr. Tappin and wondered

why Christina never picked up on the fact that Tucker simply didn't care about the things she did. It was obvious to everyone else, yet Christina acted clueless. Trisha gazed pensively out the car window. Cold, white moonlight sparkled off the fields of crusty snow. Trees in the open fields poked bare, lonely branches into the dark sky. Trisha wondered where they'd all be in the fall when they started college. Would she and Cody be together at Indiana University? Would Christina really be married to Tucker?

The Henderson High School gym was lit up and the parking lot full by the time they arrived. Inside the gym, the air felt stuffy and the noise level was deafening. The bleachers were packed on both sides. Behind the Mooresville bench sat a row of guys, some stripped to the waist, painted with the school colors—half of their bodies bright red, the other half yellow. Others wore painted stripes on their faces, like warriors about to go into battle.

Impressed by the show of school spirit, Trisha saw Frank and his girlfriend, Abby, busy taking photos for the yearbook. She waved, thinking the pictures would make a nice spread in the sports section. Cody took her hand, and they climbed up into the seniors' cheering section, stopping every few rows to say hi to friends. By the time the four of them were settled, the tip-off had brought the crowd to its feet.

The game seesawed between the two teams; at half time, Henderson led by only two points. Trisha and Christina took off to the bathroom. On the way back to their seats, they ran into Bill Lawler, who almost spilled his soda down the front of Christina's clothes. "Sorry," he mumbled, his neck and ears turning beet red.

"I wasn't watching where I was going," Christina replied, offering a smile. "How've you been?"

Bill looked at Christina with such adoration that Trisha felt embarrassed for him. He wasn't much to look at and he definitely wasn't high on the popularity list at Mooresville, but she knew Christina's kindness was sincere. "I—I've been all right," Bill said. "I got accepted to MIT. Physics is what—"

Bill stopped midsentence as he was grabbed and whirled around by his shoulder. He dropped his soda.

"What're you saying to my girl?" Tucker growled. "I told you to stay away from her." He shoved Bill against the wall behind the bleachers, stopping the flow of foot traffic.

"N-nothing—" Bill stammered, looking terrified.

"Tucker! Stop it!" Christina seized Tucker's elbow, but he sent her spinning backward into Trisha, who yelped.

From the blocked crowd, someone yelled "Fight!" and others took up the chant.

Tucker picked Bill up by his lapels. "I should take your head off, you little creep."

Christina stood horrified. Trisha said, "For crying out loud, Tucker, back off."

Bill twitched. The crowd closed in. From the middle of it, Cody shouldered his way through, caught Tucker around the neck in an iron grip, and broke his hold on Bill. "Come on, buddy. Let's cool off."

Tucker struggled briefly with Cody, but Cody wouldn't let go. "I'm going to kick his—"

"No, you're not," Cody said. "You're going to listen to me."

A commotion from the back was causing the crowd to shift and divide. "Clear the way!" a commanding voice shouted. A large, burly man came toward them. "What's the problem here? You let go, kid, or I'll call the cops." He took hold of Cody, breaking his grip on Tucker.

"He didn't do anything wrong," Trisha insisted, throwing herself in front of the man. "He was helping."

The man ignored her. He glared at Cody. "Sure he was. I think you'd better get out of here," he said. He pushed Cody toward an exit.

"But he didn't do anything!" Trisha hurried to keep up. "You've got to listen. It was the other guy." Where was Tucker and why didn't he 'fess up?

The man kept moving, herding Cody along. The crowd dispersed like scurrying ants. On the court, a roar went up as the referee blew his whistle to start the second half. The man ushering Cody stopped at the door, shoved the handle, and pushed the door open. Cold, biting air rushed in, hitting Trisha in the face.

"Now you go on," the man said to Cody. "We won't have problems here at Henderson with the likes of you."

Trisha followed Cody out into the cold, and

the steel door snapped shut behind them. She stood shivering, angry tears stinging her eyes. "He wouldn't even listen! That man just ignored me when I tried to tell him this was all Tucker's fault."

Cody put his arms around Trisha. "It's okay," he said into her hair, but she felt the tension in his body, heard a tremor in his voice. "You're freezing." He rubbed his hands up and down her arms.

"He didn't even give us a chance to get our coats," Trisha grumbled.

Trisha heard someone calling her name and looked over Cody's shoulder to see Christina running toward them. Tucker jogged behind her. Christina arrived breathless. She tossed Trisha her coat. "Are you two all right?" Christina had jammed on a ski hat and her blond hair stuck out from the sides.

"We're fine," Cody said, helping Trisha on with her coat.

"No thanks to Tucker!" Trisha whirled to face him. "Thanks for standing up for your friend! Thanks for nothing!"

"Hey, man, I'm sorry, but I got shoved away." He handed Cody his coat. "That guy was a real jerk! He took you away before I could say a word."

"Oh, right!" Trisha said sarcastically. "Like you even tried to straighten things out."

"It wouldn't have mattered," Cody said over their raised voices. "We were toast the second Tucker took a swing at Bill."

"You had no right to do that." Christina's voice cut through the night. "Why would you do such a thing? Bill's no threat to you."

Tucker clenched his fists. "I told him to stay away from you. I told him I didn't even want to see him within ten feet of you."

"That's stupid," Christina shot back.

"Don't call me stupid." Tucker stepped toward her, but Christina held her ground.

"What you did was stupid," she said. "You don't own me, Tucker."

"Can we take this to the car?" Cody asked. "Trisha and I are freezing."

Tucker stomped off, heading to the parking lot.

Christina turned to Trisha and Cody. "I—I don't know what to say . . ."

"It's not your fault," Trisha said. "Just remember this the next time Tucker lights into you. Is this what you want, Chrissy? To always be wondering what's going to set him off? Is this what being in love with Tucker means?"

Christina hugged her arms to her chest, looking sad. "I'm cold."

"Come on," Cody said, putting an arm around each girl and moving them toward the parked car. "We can't solve the problem here. We'll go someplace warm. Eat. Talk it out."

To Trisha, the time for talking was past. Tucker would never change. Christina needed to be rid of him.

Tucker had started the car while they crossed the parking lot. When the others were settled inside, he reached for Christina. She pushed him away. "Don't."

"I said I was sorry."

"That's what you always say, but you never change."

"Just don't be mad at me, baby. I went crazy when I saw him talking to you. I love you so much. I don't know what gets into me."

Christina said nothing.

In the backseat, Trisha wrapped the blanket tightly around her and Cody. But in spite of the blanket and Cody pressed against her, she couldn't get warm. Tucker had ruined the whole evening.

"Let's go back to town and stop at the Pizza Hut," Cody said.

"Good idea." Tucker brightened and put the car in gear. He pulled out of the parking lot and started toward Mooresville.

Tucker switched on the radio and turned the music up loud. Trisha watched Christina from the back. She could tell that her friend was holding her neck and shoulders rigid, which gave her hope that this time Tucker had finally gone over the top. Maybe now she would leave him.

The car cruised down the long, straight highway. The snowy, vacant fields flew past. Trisha saw a flash of headlights in the rearview mirror. She blinked.

"What's this guy's problem?" Tucker asked, glancing over his shoulder at the car.

Cody and Trisha straightened up and looked through the back window. A car seemed to be sitting on their bumper.

"I'll lose him," Tucker said, giving the car more gas.

"Don't," Christina said.

"He's jamming us."

"So what?" said Cody.

The car pulled up alongside them, keeping even with their bumper as the group of kids inside waved at them. A boy in the front passenger seat made gestures. "What's he doing?" Trisha asked.

"Acting cute," Cody said. "Ignore them. Hey, Tuck, back off, okay?"

As Tucker slowed, the other car cut in front of them and slowed dramatically.

Trisha looked through the front windshield and saw taillights coming up fast.

Tucker slammed on the brake. "This guy's begging for trouble."

"Don't, Tucker," Christina said. "Let them go on."

Tucker blasted the horn, and one of the riders in the other car made a rude gesture through the back window. "I'm passing him."

"Back off," Cody said. "Besides, he'll just speed up again if you try."

Tucker pulled out to pass. "Basic physics, my man—force equals mass times acceleration."

Trisha saw the front car's taillights brighten as it slowed. She gripped Cody's hand.

"No! Don't!" Christina cried.

A sick sensation seized Trisha and for the

space of a few seconds, she felt as if the car had grown wings and they were flying. Then, suddenly, the world turned upside down. Glass rained down. Metal tore. Someone screamed. The world went dark.

Five

❧❦

Trisha swam in a sea of blackness, her body icy cold. From somewhere, music blared. *If Charlie doesn't turn down his CD player, Mom's going to kill him*, she thought. She tried to move, searching for her bed covers and longing to feel warm. She seemed weighted down but didn't know why. *Turn off the music, Charlie.* . . .

She jolted awake. She lay on a blanket of snow. Her cheek felt wet, her legs numb. Light arced from behind her, throwing white spotlights on the snow in front of her face. She moaned and pulled herself upward to her knees. A wave of nausea made her gag. The music wouldn't stop. She saw a field of snow, blue-white in the moonlight. Moisture dripped from her lip and cheek. She tried to remember what happened, but a voice interrupted her thoughts.

"Don't move," someone said. "Help's coming."

She staggered to her feet anyway. A hand reached out to steady her. She saw a boy her age, his face pale and white in the moonlight. "Who . . . ?" was all she could manage.

"You've been in a wreck. We were in the car you tried to pass. The car you were in went off the road and . . . and it flipped."

She turned just enough to see that the arc of light was coming from the headlights of an overturned car. The vehicle looked like some giant's toy, lying on its roof, its metal underbelly exposed to the cold night.

"I used my cell phone in the car—the paramedics are on their way. You should stay put," the boy said.

She moved past him as if he hadn't spoken, and tried to make sense of the jagged landscape. She needed to find Cody. Where was he? He wouldn't have gone away and left her. Except for being cold, she felt nothing. The music kept blaring. Why didn't someone turn it off?

"Here, you need a coat." The boy moved beside her, putting his jacket around her shoulders. It didn't make her feel any warmer.

Trisha started toward the car, but the boy turned her away. The doors were thrown open, the windshield smashed, the seats crushed, empty. Her eyes began to water. From far away, she heard the sound of a siren. It came closer, and soon eerie red lights splayed across the field of snow. She took a step. Heavy snow crunched and clung to her new boots. Trisha peered down at her boots, suddenly worried about them. If they were damaged, her mother was going to be so mad at her. Trisha remembered her mother saying, "Can't you wear your old ones tonight? Save these for Sunday?"

She had replied, "No, Mom, I can't. Why have new boots if I can't wear them?"

Her tights were shredded, but the boots looked fine. She was glad they weren't ruined, then wondered why it should matter. The car was mangled and shattered and she was worrying about her stupid boots!

"Sit down and wait for help," the boy beside her said.

"I'm fine," she said, surprised at how calm

her voice sounded. "Do you know where my friends are? A girl and two guys. Did they go off without me?"

Out of the night, a man carrying a large white box came toward her through the snow. "Take it easy," he said. "I'm a paramedic. I'm going to help you."

"I'm so cold," she said.

He got her to the door of the ambulance, where she saw Tucker sitting on the running board. He held a towel against his forehead. His shirt was ripped, and a cut ran from his shoulder to his elbow. "Are you all right?" Tucker asked.

"I—I think so." She glanced around, confused. "Where's Cody? And Christina?"

"Don't know."

A rolling stretcher had materialized, and two men lifted her onto it. "No," she said. "I don't need that. I'm fine."

The paramedics ignored her, strapped her onto a backboard, and immobilized her head.

"Stop it!" she said, trying to move. She felt pinned in place, like an insect skewered to a display case.

"Lie still," the medic said. "You're in shock. Don't move. You could hurt yourself more."

She didn't believe him. She didn't feel a thing.

Police cars came with screaming sirens and whirling blue lights, and where their lights melded with the red lights of the emergency units, the snow looked purple. Doors opened, and more medics emerged. Someone shined a bright light into her eyes and snapped, "Responsive. Let's get an IV in her and transport her."

Something stung the back of her hand, and a bag was hung on a metal pole on the stretcher. "Cody. Where's Cody?" she asked. "And where's Christina?"

"Have you been drinking?" a paramedic asked. "Any drugs?"

"No." How could they think such a thing?

Tucker bent over her, took her free hand. "It's okay, Trisha."

Tears were sliding down the sides of her face. She wanted to wipe them but couldn't move. Tucker brushed them away for her. "I'll be in the ambulance with you. We're together, you hear?"

The stretcher began to move. Hands lifted it into the ambulance. As the stretcher rose, she saw shapes in a ditch, sprawled out like broken dolls. Just a glimpse, an impression, but one doll looked twisted, the other wore a ski hat. The sound of a scream filled her ears. It was a full minute before she realized it was hers.

In the ambulance, the paramedic asked her name and began to check her body. "Trisha, does anything hurt?"

"My head."

"You've got a nasty cut that'll probably need stitches," he said, applying a bandage to the top of her head. She winced when he manipulated her right knee. Because her head was immobilized, all she could move were her eyes. She moved them in all directions. Lights glowed down from the metal top of the vehicle and rows of shelves crammed with medical equipment and paraphernalia lined the inside. She saw Tucker sitting on a bench; another medic was taking his blood pressure.

She asked, "Tucker, what happened to us?"

"Ice. We hit a patch of ice, and the car fishtailed. I tried to keep it on the road, but I couldn't." Tucker's voice shook as he explained.

"What about the others?"

He shrugged. "I blacked out and when I came to, I was still inside the car. The kids that stopped . . . they helped me out. I—I didn't see the others."

Just as Trisha started to tell him she thought she had, the paramedic began to cut off her sweater with a pair of shears. "Do you have to? I—I'm cold," she said.

"I have to check you," he said.

She felt mortified, lying on a stretcher, unable to move, her clothing being peeled off her body in layers. "Can't it wait?"

"The ER doc's going to want to know as much as possible when we get there. Your clothes could be hiding an injury."

She shut her eyes, seeing her mother's face in her mind's eye. All at once, she wanted her mother desperately. She wanted her mother to hold her and tell her everything was going to be all right. "My parents. They need to know. Who's going to tell them? I want to talk to them—"

"The hospital will call them."

Feeling sick to her stomach again, she squeezed her eyes tighter shut and prayed that she wouldn't throw up. She couldn't believe this was happening, this nightmare from which she couldn't wake up. "The others in the car," she said to the medic, "do you know what happened to them?"

"Another ambulance is bringing them in. Can you tell me where else you hurt?"

"My cheek and my lip."

He bent over, examining her mouth through narrowed eyes. "You've got glass imbedded in your lip. They'll remove it in the ER. Try not to talk."

She shuddered at the idea of glass ground into her face.

The ambulance pulled into the unloading zone for the emergency room and the doors popped open. Her stretcher was removed from the ambulance, and she was transferred to another. Blankets were thrown over her. Inside the building, she was wheeled into a large, brightly lit room and parked behind a curtain. "Hi, Trisha," a slim, dark-haired woman said, glancing at a chart the paramedic had handed her. "I'm Dr. Joyce. Do you know what happened to you?"

"We had a car wreck."

"What do you remember?"

"I—I'm not sure. I saw taillights. The car

began flying . . ." She shut her eyes. The effort
to remember was making her head hurt worse.
"I—I woke up and I was lying in the snow. I
had friends in the car too. Do you know—"

"We're going to stitch up your head, then
take some X rays," Dr. Joyce said, cutting
Trisha off. She pulled back the curtain and
barked at a tech, "Let's get this one stitched
and into radiology. I want head and torso
shots. Give me a look at her right knee too."

Another doctor appeared. He tried to
soothe her as he ripped open a small kit that
held scissors, needles, and surgical thread. "I'm
pretty good at this," he said with a reassuring
smile. "First I'll dab on some numbing gel, then
give you a shot of lidocaine. You won't feel
anything." He picked up the scissors. "I'm going to have to cut your hair, though."

"Don't . . ." She'd been trying to grow it
long because Cody liked long hair.

"I have to, miss. It's just hair—it will grow
back." He set to work.

When he was finished, an orderly came, and
as she was being wheeled down the hall, she
caught a glimpse of her reflection in a convex
mirror hanging in the corridor. Could that be

her? Blood caked the side of her face and matted her hair. Her lip looked distorted, and one eye was almost swollen shut. She stifled the urge to scream.

In radiology, a technician instructed her to lie still while he framed up a machine that scanned her body and took X rays from various angles. The machine looked monstrous to her, not at all like the tiny cone-shaped device her dentist used to take photos of her teeth. She wanted her parents more than anything. She wanted someone to talk to her and tell her about her friends. When she was through, an ER tech took her back to triage in the emergency room. She passed Tucker, who was being wheeled on a stretcher toward radiology. His head was wrapped in a bandage. She was too scared to speak. Where was Cody? And Christina?

Dr. Joyce's face loomed over Trisha. "Your parents are on the way," she said, patting Trisha's arm. "I'll be back just as soon as your X rays are developed and I check them out."

"I hate being tied down," Trisha whispered hoarsely, straining against her restraints.

"It's only a precaution. If nothing's broken,

I'll remove the backboard. A nurse will be over in a minute to start cleaning you up. You may need stitches in that cheek; if you do, I'll call Dr. Scanland. She's a plastic surgeon and does good work. Your face is too young and pretty to scar." The doctor said all this with a smile that brought Trisha no comfort. Dr. Joyce closed the curtain halfway as she left.

Suddenly, Trisha was alone with only the noise of clattering equipment and disembodied voices. The smell of antiseptic and alcohol hung in the warm air. She felt her eyelids growing heavy but fought against the urge to sleep. She heard the sound of her own blood in her ears, felt tears slide down her cheeks. Her skin stung when the warm, salty fluid hit her wounds.

She heard the noise of a stretcher being moved and darted her eyes toward the sound. Through a gap in the curtain, she saw a man dressed in hospital garb walk away from the rolling bed he had parked out of the way along a wall. A sheet covered the form of a body on the bed. A hand hung downward just under the edge of the sheet. The fingers never moved. Trisha's breath caught. *Dear God . . .* The person on the stretcher was dead. Trisha knew it deep inside her gut. She began to shake uncontrollably.

All at once, the curtain was shoved aside and her mother's voice cut through the void. "Trisha! Oh, my baby . . . my dear, sweet baby. Look at me, honey. Talk to me, please."

Six

~❧~

"Mama . . . oh, Mama, I'm so glad you're here." Trisha broke into sobs as relief flooded through her.

"Of course I'm here, baby. We got here as soon as we could."

"Where's Dad?"

"Here, sweetheart."

Her father took her hand. The world righted itself, and Trisha didn't feel so scared and alone.

"I'm here too." Trisha looked over and saw Charlie's pinched, white face. "Are you okay, Trisha? I mean really and truly okay?"

"I think so."

Charlie's eyes were wet. "The police came to our house and told us you were in an acci-

dent. I thought—I was scared you might be—"
His voice cracked.

All the feelings of annoyance she'd ever
held toward him vanished in a wave of tender-
ness. She put herself in his place and realized
she would be frantic if he were on this table
instead of her. "I'm all right, Charlie. Honest."

He touched her tentatively, as if he wasn't
positive she had real form and substance. "Can
you come home with us?"

She didn't answer because a nurse appeared, and her family's faces receded as they
moved aside. "Let me clean up your daughter,"
the nurse said kindly. "Take a seat in the waiting room and I'll tell Dr. Joyce you're here."

To Trisha, the cleanup was long and painful.
Peering through a magnifying glass, the nurse
extracted pieces of broken glass from Trisha's
lip and cheek. Then she cleaned the area with
an antiseptic that stung like fire, smoothed on
ointment, and placed a soft dressing across the
cheek. "It doesn't look like you'll need stitches
on your face. It's just a bad scrape—you know,
like when you were a kid and fell off your bike
and skinned your knee. That ever happen
to you?"

Trisha sniffed.

"You're going to have a fat lip for a few days, though. And maybe a black eye. But your face will heal nicely."

"Do you know about the others from the accident?"

"Not yet," the nurse said.

"I—I saw one of my friends being taken to X ray, but the others . . . no one will tell me about the others. Didn't an ambulance bring them in? You see, one of them is my boyfriend and the other is my best friend." Just asking about her friends was making Trisha cry.

The nurse patted her shoulder. "Now, now. Calm down. I'll check with Dr. Joyce for you, all right?"

"They should be here, you know. I mean, they should be if they're . . . okay." She couldn't bring herself to offer any other explanation.

"I'll see if Dr. Joyce wants me to give you a little something to calm you," the nurse said, then left.

Moments later, Dr. Joyce swung the curtain aside. "Good news, Trisha. I've looked at your X rays and they look good. That means we can remove the backboard. You wanted that, didn't you?"

Trisha agreed, and when it was gone, she felt freed from a prison.

"You're going to be very sore for a few days," Dr. Joyce said. "You'll need to keep your knee wrapped for a couple of weeks and you'll need crutches to get around for a while. Your family doctor can remove the stitches from your head in a week. You're very lucky."

"Can I go home?"

"I want to keep you a few more hours for observation. After all, you were knocked unconscious, and we always like to keep a close eye on head injuries. However, I'll be giving you something to relax you, and that will make the time pass faster."

"Can my parents stay with me?" She dreaded the thought of being alone—even if she was drugged.

"I'll send in your mother. There's really not enough room for everybody."

The nurse came and stuck a syringe into the IV line; within seconds, Trisha felt light-headed and fuzzy. By the time her mother materialized, Trisha felt as if she were floating off the table. "Mom . . . ," she mumbled.

"Don't talk," her mother said. "Dr. Joyce has

explained everything to us and said that right now, you need your rest."

"What . . . time . . . ?"

"It's two A.M. I sent your dad home with Charlie." Her mother pulled a chair alongside the bed and circled Trisha's head with her arm. "Trisha, we were all so scared. Thank God you weren't injured any worse. We talked to the police who were at the scene. They said that it didn't look like you were wearing your seat belt. Is that true? Didn't you have it on?"

She flipped through mental pictures. She remembered getting into the car in the Henderson High School parking lot. She'd been upset and angry at Tucker. She remembered sliding into the seat next to Cody. She recalled him putting his arm around her and settling the blanket across their laps. She didn't remember snapping her seat belt into place. "I—I don't think so," she confessed.

"Oh, Trisha, why not?" Her mother's face had a terrible expression. "You know better."

It was true. Trisha had taken driver's ed in school and she'd watched the horrific videos of accident victims who hadn't worn their seat belts. "P-please don't be mad at me . . ."

Her mother sniffed hard. "I'm not mad,

honey, just so scared. Tucker was wearing his belt. That's why he wasn't thrown from the car, according to the police. Evidently no one else was wearing a belt. No one. And all of you should have been."

Trisha recalled being lifted into the ambulance and catching sight of two bodies lying in a ditch. She hadn't imagined it. The bodies had been Cody's and Christina's. She struggled to stay awake just a little bit longer. "Tell me about Cody. Are his parents here too?"

Her mother looked straight into Trisha's eyes and smoothed her shorn hair, careful not to touch the fresh stitches. "Cody's been taken to a Chicago hospital."

"Chicago? B-but why so far away?" Trisha's thoughts drifted to Labor Day weekend, when she and Christina had ridden the train into the city to shop the department store sales. They had stayed until the stores closed and almost missed the train home. She remembered how they'd collapsed, breathless and laughing, onto the seats just as the train pulled out of the station. On the ride home, they'd played show-and-tell, each taking turns to admire their purchases.

"Here's my favorite," Christina said. She held

up a pale blue twinset that perfectly matched her eyes. "*I'm going to wear it for a very special occasion.*"

"*Which will be . . . ?*"

"*Don't know yet. But when you see it on me, you'll know it's a special day.*"

Trisha's thoughts floated back to the present. Again she asked, "Why is Cody being sent to Chicago?"

"He's had a massive head injury. Chicago is better able to take care of him because the hospital has a special head trauma unit."

Trisha's heart seemed to contract. "How bad is he hurt? Tell me, Mom . . . please tell me."

Her mother hesitated but finally said, "He has a couple of broken ribs. And his face and arm needed stitches."

"That doesn't sound too bad."

Her mother paused.

"What else? What aren't you telling me?"

"He's in a coma, honey."

Trisha felt all the air go out of her lungs. "A coma? What does that mean?"

"I'm not sure."

"Oh, no . . . Not Cody, not Cody." Hot tears pooled behind her eyes.

"Please don't get upset. It won't help you."

"Me? I don't care about me. I'll be fine. But Cody . . ." She cried just thinking about him far away in a hospital, without her by his side. "Please tell me everything."

"I was standing with his parents and heard what the doctor told them. He said that comas are nature's way of protecting the brain. Cody could wake up tomorrow."

"I want to be there when he wakes up."

"We have no way of knowing when that will be. But I'll take you to see him just as soon as you're able."

"But what if he doesn't wake up?"

"They're doing everything they can for him, Trisha. Don't dwell on the negatives."

"I want to see him."

"You will. Just as soon as you're able to travel."

"I want to see him now."

"That's not possible, honey." Her mother kissed her forehead. "Pray for him. Think good thoughts for him. That's all you can do right now."

"Can I call his mother?"

"Tomorrow. There's time enough for that tomorrow."

Trisha lay quiet for a while, concentrating

on the vision of Cody's face. His smile lit up his eyes and made them crinkle at the corners. She loved it when he came up behind her in the halls, put his arm around her shoulder, and whispered in her ear, "Who loves you, babe?"

And she'd say, "Have we met?"

And he'd say, "Don't tell me you're spoken for. Am I going to have to take some guy out before we can live happily ever after?"

And she'd say, "No. You're the one I want."

"Forever?"

"Forever."

Trisha's eyelids grew heavy, but she fought sleep. She still hadn't heard about Christina. She clenched and unclenched her hands, digging her nails into her palms, psyching herself up to hear the news. "And Christina, Mom? How's Christina?"

"You know, there'll be plenty of time to talk tomorrow. You should get some rest now. I'll go find Dr. Joyce and see if I can take you home." Her mother stood.

"Wait." Trisha caught her arm, her heart hammering hard. "Tell me about Christina. I don't want to leave here until I know. If she's really bad, I want to see her before I go."

Her mother's eyes filled with tears, but she

held Trisha's gaze without blinking. "I didn't want to tell you this tonight. I wanted to wait until you were rested, stronger."

Trisha felt new tears forming in her eyes and braced herself for what was to come, for what she could not change.

"Christina died at the scene, Trisha," her mother said. "Chrissy's dead."

Seven

Deep down, Trisha had known all along. She had felt it in her soul. When had she first suspected it? Perhaps when she'd been lifted into the ambulance and seen the dark shapes in the ditch. Or when she'd glimpsed the stretcher along the wall, the sheet pulled up to cover the human being beneath it. Her subconscious had seen it in the graceful shape of the arm, the limp fingers, the curve of the hand. Trisha had known on some primal inner level that of the four of them, someone had not survived.

Tears clogged Trisha's throat, yet she wept without making a sound. She might have choked had her mother not shaken her and made her cough and take a ragged breath. "I'm sorry, honey. I'm so very, very sorry."

Trisha turned and pressed her face into her mother's stomach, her sobs muffled against her mother's clothes. Her mother held her tight and stroked her back. Together they cried until Trisha was so exhausted that her body sagged, almost as lifeless as her friend's. How could it be true? How could Christina, so full of life hours before, be dead and gone? And what of Tucker? He must know by now too.

She thought about what he must be going through if he knew. What was it like for him, knowing that he had been driving the car that killed the girl he loved?

"You don't have to go to school today, Trisha."

"Yes, Mom, I do." While she hobbled awkwardly on her crutches, gathering her books for her backpack, Trisha never looked at her mother standing in the doorway of her room. "And this would go a whole lot faster if you'd help me out a little," she added, feeling frustrated.

"Why is it so important for you to head off to school less than two days after your accident? It's only Monday. Your teachers will understand if you stay out for the entire week. There's no need to rush back."

"I can't stay out. I have to go. Because of Christina." She almost broke down just saying the name.

She'd come home from the hospital early Saturday morning, gone to bed, and slept until almost two in the afternoon. She'd awakened with a start, wondering why her parents had let her sleep so late. As she moved, pain shot through her. Only then did she remember what had happened. She'd gotten up, found the crutches the ER issued her, and made it down the hallway to the bathroom. When she saw herself in the mirror, she almost fainted.

Her hair had been cut away and a large bald spot shaved where black stitches crisscrossed part of her head. Her face was swollen, her lip bulged, and the area under her left eye was bruised black. Dried blood was caked in her hair and on her neck. She was Frankenstein's monster.

Too sore even to begin cleaning up, she returned to her room. She thought about calling

Christina's mother, but couldn't bring herself to do it. Later, she had been relieved when her mother had told her that she had called, but that Christina's family had left a message on their answering machine saying, "We are not taking calls at this time, but we appreciate your condolences. Please give us a few days alone with our grief." No one was home at Cody's house when she called, but later that night, his mother, Gwyn, returned Trisha's message. "How is he?" Trisha asked, emotion filling her voice.

"He's still in a coma," Gwyn said. "But he's breathing on his own. That's a good thing." Her voice quivered. "I just want him to wake up."

"Did they tell you when he might?"

"They don't know. They said comas can be healing to the brain. Cody's head has suffered a severe injury and the coma is a way for it to rest and recover."

"I want to see him so badly."

"And I didn't want to come home and leave him there," Gwyn said. "But I have to take care of Jennifer and Pete." Those were Cody's siblings. "We'll all go to Chicago tomorrow and visit. He looks so pitiful in the bed. He can't speak. He can't even open his eyes."

The picture was too much for Trisha to bear. "Maybe I can come too."

"Wait a while," Gwyn said. "Maybe he'll wake up in a day or so. Then you can come. How are you, anyway?"

Trisha told her about her injuries, finishing with "I look terrible, but I'm all right. I mean, compared to Cody and to—" She stopped herself as tears welled.

"Yes, yes. I know. I think of Christina's family all the time. I know Julia and Nelson are devastated." Gwyn was silent, then added, "I'll call you the minute there's any change in Cody. In the meantime, take care of yourself."

By Monday, the swelling on Trisha's face had gone down and she could cover the ugly bruising around her eye with makeup. With little fanfare, she'd chopped off her hair. She found a knit hat she liked, which she wore brim down. Struggling into jeans and a sweater, she prepared to go to school.

"I really wish you'd take another few days off," her mother said, helping Trisha down the stairs and into the kitchen.

Charlie looked up from where he sat at the kitchen table and jumped to his feet. "Here, take my chair." He pulled it out so that she could sit. "Want my cereal? I only took a couple of bites."

"No thanks." She tried to smile at him, but her lip throbbed too much.

"You must eat something," their mother said. "I won't let you leave until you eat breakfast."

Food was the last thing Trisha wanted, but she didn't want to give her mother an excuse to keep her home. "Can I have toast with peanut butter? And maybe some milk."

As her mother set to work, Trisha let Charlie prop her crutches against the wall. "You going to school?" he asked. "You can stay home if you want. If it was me, I'd stay home."

"I'm not you."

The morning paper was spread across the table, open to the local news section. Christina's pretty face smiled from a photo and the headline read: *Mooresville Teen Dies in Crash; Three Injured*. Trisha all but stopped breathing when she read the word *dies*.

"I told you to put that paper away!" Her mother barked at Charlie.

He looked panic-stricken and reached for

the paper. Trisha stopped him. "Don't. Please. I—I want to read it."

"I'm sorry," Charlie mumbled.

"It's not your fault," she told him.

She picked up the paper. At the bottom was a photograph of rescue personnel and police standing around a car resting on its squashed roof. Had a news reporter been at the scene? Trisha didn't remember. With difficulty, she read the article:

A seventeen-year-old Mooresville High School student was killed Friday night in a one-car accident on State Highway 2, just outside the city limits, when the car she was a passenger in left the road, crashed through a fence, and overturned. Christina Eckloe, daughter of Nelson and Julia Eckloe, was transported to Memorial Hospital, where she died of injuries sustained in the wreck.

Two other passengers, Trisha Thompson, 17, and Cody McGuire, 17, and driver Tucker Hanson, 18, were transported to Memorial, where Ms. Thompson and Mr. Hanson were treated and released. Mr. McGuire was transferred to Chicago for treatment of head injuries. Mr. Hanson was driving the vehicle, but police have not charged him, and the investigation into the accident is ongoing.

The Reverend Jonathon Stiles, pastor of the church Miss Eckloe and her family attended, spoke on behalf of the family, saying, "Christina was a warm and wonderful girl. She was loved and admired by the whole community and will be greatly missed." (See obituary on page 7.)

Trisha stopped reading. Her hands shook so hard that she couldn't hold the paper steady. "Would you turn it to page seven?" she asked Charlie.

He glanced up at their mother, who gave a resigned nod.

In the obituary section, Christina smiled from her senior picture. Trisha noted the particulars about Christina's funeral listed beside the photo. "The visitation's tonight," she said with a start, looking hard at her mother. "Weren't you going to tell me? Were you going to let me miss it?"

"Of course not."

Trisha didn't believe her. "And the funeral's Tuesday. Were you going to let me skip that too?"

"There's time—"

"Time? Time for what? She's dead, Mother. My best friend's dead and you weren't even going to let me go to her funeral."

"That's not true—"

Trisha cried out and swept the paper from the table. She struggled to her feet. "I hate you! I hate all of you!"

Charlie looked dumbstruck. Their mother rushed over to Trisha and caught her by the arms. "Stop it! We would have never let you miss the funeral. We only wanted to protect you. Now get ahold of yourself."

Trisha dissolved into heartrending sobs. Her mother cradled her. "She's gone, Mama. She's gone forever. What am I going to do? What am I going to do?"

Her mother didn't answer, and Trisha knew there was no answer. Christina was dead. In two days she'd be buried. She'd be put into the hard cold ground, never to see the world again.

"Why don't you lie down?" her mother said.

Trisha pulled away. "I'm going to school,"

she said. "Someone has to be there for Christina today. And if you won't take me, I swear, I'll walk every step of the way."

She didn't have to walk. Her mother got her to the front entrance; as Trisha slowly made her way through the halls, groups of kids parted like field grass to let her pass. They stared. Ordinarily, the stares and whispers would have made her feel self-conscious. Today she didn't. Because today, it wasn't about her. It was about Christina. She heard the name spoken as she passed, from voices filled with tears. She didn't say a word to anyone because she didn't trust her voice.

Heading toward her locker, she rounded a corner. A teacher stepped in front of her. "Trisha, you're back so soon?"

No, Mrs. Dodge, I'm only a figment of your imagination. "Yes, Mrs. Dodge. I couldn't stay home. Not today."

"It's all so tragic. I'm glad you weren't hurt any worse."

Any worse than my heart being ripped in half? "Thank you, Mrs. Dodge."

"And Cody? How's he doing?"

He could have died too, Mrs. Dodge. We were

all just a heartbeat away from dying in the accident like Christina. "His doctors don't know yet." Trisha wished the woman would go away.

"We're going to have a memorial service in the gym on Friday," Mrs. Dodge said. "We decided at an emergency faculty meeting this morning. We think it will give the school a chance to pay their respects to Christina and gain closure. Since you knew her best, we thought you might like to say a few words. Can we count on you, Trisha?"

A service? A rally? A send-off? Are you joking? Trisha felt numb. "I—I guess I could."

"I told the staff it would be all right to ask you." Mrs. Dodge turned. "We're all sorry, Trisha. She was a wonderful girl." Mrs. Dodge patted Trisha's shoulder and walked off.

Was. Used to be. Once upon a time. Christina was past tense. Trisha's chest felt as if a heavy weight were pressing into it. She went lightheaded. The floor began to spin. She dropped her crutches. A hand grabbed her. She looked up into Tucker's grief-stricken face.

"Let me help you," he said.

She had no choice—her knees had started to cave in. Without warning, a wail rose from her throat. Tucker put his arms around her, and they stood in the hall clinging to one another, crying. A group of students held hands and closed ranks around them, as if to shield them from the tentacles of a monster they could not escape.

Eight

❧

Trisha and Tucker were taken to the guidance counselor's office by a teacher who found them crying together and believed they should "take it easy" and that perhaps they had returned to school too soon after their "ordeal." And that maybe meeting with Mr. Chambers might help them "get a handle" on their emotions. Trisha wanted none of it. She felt bad about breaking down so publicly, but she didn't want her mother called. And she didn't want to talk to Mr. Chambers about it either.

To Mr. Chambers's credit, he didn't push either Trisha or Tucker to talk. He brought them both colas from the drink machine and, after a few minutes of making sure neither Trisha nor Tucker was hysterical or totally undone, he left them alone. Trisha hadn't seen Tucker since the night of the accident. He wore a large, flesh-colored bandage on his right temple where his head had struck the windshield. There was another bandage on his forearm; Trisha saw it under the edge of his sleeve. His eyes were red-rimmed. He had cried. She had seen Charlie cry, but he was a kid and Tucker wasn't. She thought better of Tucker because he had cried instead of clinging to some stoic macho code.

"How are you doing?" Tucker spoke first.

"Not so good. How about you?"

"The same. My parents didn't want me to come to school today."

"My mom wanted me to stay home too."

"My dad thinks everyone's going to blame me. Do you blame me, Trisha?"

She didn't know how to answer him. His expression was one of pure torture, but truth was, he had been driving the car. She thought hard before saying, "I don't remember much about the accident, you know. It's mostly just impressions—a flash here and there, pictures that keep rolling around inside my head that I can't quite pin down."

" 'Cause I couldn't stand it if you thought it was my fault. I wouldn't blame you, but I couldn't stand it."

"The paper didn't say much about the accident. Did you read the story?"

"I read it. The police told us there'll be a coroner's inquest into the accident. That's where they'll decide if it was an accident or a reckless homicide." His voice broke. "What if it's ruled a reckless homicide, Trisha? What if they say it was my fault? That Christina's dead and Cody's in a coma because I was driving recklessly?"

She heard his pain and his fear. She couldn't believe how life had changed so quickly for them. She wanted to tell him it would be all right, but she couldn't. Something kept nibbling at the edges of her mind, some memory about the night of the accident that couldn't get out. She hated the blank spaces in her head. They gave her a headache. "I guess you'll have to go with whatever they say," she told him. And thought, *and deal with the consequences.*

"I guess so." He buried his face in his hands, rubbed his eyes, and groaned. "Why did this have to happen? She didn't deserve to die. Maybe I am guilty. Maybe it was all my fault."

She couldn't console him. She had never cared for Tucker, but now he was the only person in the world who understood what she was going through. He was part of the situation—but was he responsible? Other people might say they understood, but how could they? Had they been in the car? Had they lain in the wet snow, or heard sirens coming for them, or seen their best friend covered with a sheet in a hospital?

She and Tucker had survived. "How do you suppose God decides who lives and who dies?" she asked, not because she expected an answer, but simply because the question had popped into her mind. "Why did we live and Christina die? I'm not so special. She was very special."

"I don't know," he said. "God didn't play fair."

"I'm scared for Cody," she said. "I'm scared he might die too." She voiced her deepest fear, because she and Tucker were in this together and she *had* to tell someone what was eating her alive.

"I talked to his mother. She was nice to me. I thought she might hate me, but she doesn't," Tucker said.

Trisha couldn't grant him absolution, no matter how many times or ways he asked her for it. "I'm scared about tonight too," she said. "About the viewing and all."

"Do you think—" he stopped, then started again. "They'll make her look pretty, won't they? I mean, isn't that their job? To make people look good even after an accident?"

She hadn't thought about it, but the idea that Christina might look mangled and battered made her stomach feel queasy. "I—I guess so." Her friend was so pretty in life. Shouldn't she look the same in death?

"You'll be there, won't you?" He looked apprehensive.

"I'll be there."

"Can I hang with you? I don't want to be there by myself."

"But your parents will come, won't they?" She didn't think she could be responsible for Tucker and herself.

"Sure. But so will hers."

His message hit her like stones. She had yet to face Christina's parents. In her mind's eye, she saw Christina's pretty blond mother, Julia. She saw the years of afternoons she had spent at Christina's house, with Julia more like a third girlfriend than a mother. Christina was her parents' only child and they adored her. They were alone now. Devastated.

Trisha said, "If you get there first, wait for us in the parking lot. If I get there first, come inside and find me."

He looked grateful. Tears shimmered in his eyes. "Thanks."

It struck her that in all the years she'd known him, she'd never heard him say that word to her. "It's what Christina would have wanted," she said. "She would want us to stick together."

Trisha heard the bell ring, glanced at the clock, and was shocked to see that it was almost noon. The morning was gone. The afternoon would be gone soon too. All that remained was the night—the long, dark night at the funeral home where Christina lay, waiting for family and friends to tell her goodbye.

Fine, dry snow spit against the windshield of their van as Trisha and her family drove to the funeral home. The weatherman had predicted cold, clear, snowless skies for the next morning, the day of the funeral. Trisha sat tight-lipped during the trip, unable to get warm, even though the heater was going full blast.

"The place looks packed," her father said, turning the van into the parking lot. "I'll let you three out, park, and meet you inside."

Pale yellow light spilled from overhead mercury lamps, giving the area an eerie, surrealistic glow. Trisha scanned the parking spaces for any sign of Tucker or his family but didn't see them. She figured they hadn't arrived yet. In the lobby, a black-suited man directed them to where a crowd had gathered near a doorway to one of the parlors. A sign read MISS CHRISTINA ECKLOE. People were signing their names in a book on a podium beside the door. Trisha had attended her grandmother's funeral when she was nine, so she was familiar with viewings.

She saw kids from school everywhere she looked. Most were gathered in groups and standing with each other. Many were crying, but some were whispering to each other, even smiling and waving to friends. Where was their respect? Had they come to mourn or to see and be seen? She wanted to brandish her crutches and hit them.

She might have done it too, except that her

father came along, took her elbow, and said, "Are you ready to go in?"

She would never be ready. "Sure," she lied.

She walked between her parents, with Charlie close behind, into the dimly lit room. She saw Julia dressed in black, her hair pulled back in a severe bun. She wore no makeup. "Trisha!" Julia pulled Trisha into her arms, weeping. "My heart's broken, Trisha. I can't believe she's gone."

Over Julia's shoulder, Trisha saw the front of the room, where a red velvet curtain hung and a gleaming pale blue casket sat on a black-draped table. Hundreds of flowers in vases, wreaths, baskets, and display panels flanked the table. More flowers lined both sides of the room. Trisha could hardly breathe in the warm perfumed air. It felt oppressive, suffocating.

Julia pulled away. "Let me take you to see her," she said.

Panic raced down Trisha's spine. "I—I don't—"

"She looks pretty," Christina's father, Nelson, said. "Don't be alarmed."

Trisha's mother stepped to her other side and laid her hand on Trisha's shoulder. "We'll be right here with you, honey."

Trembling, heart hammering, Trisha made her way to the front between the two mothers. The top portion of the casket was raised and locked into place. There, on a bed of creamy white satin, lay Christina. Her hair, long and sleek, fanned onto a satin pillow. Trisha was startled to see that she was dressed in the pale blue cashmere sweater set she'd bought on the Labor Day shopping trip to Chicago. A tiny gold cross on a chain twinkled on her neck, its small diamond flashing with cold, white fire. Her hands were crossed demurely at her waist and held a single white calla lilly. She looked for all the world like a princess gone to sleep, as if waiting for some magical prince to kiss her and wake her up.

Trisha half expected Christina to sit up, look around the room, and ask why everyone was crying. She did not. For all her beauty Christina's skin had a waxen quality. Her cheeks were colored an artificial shade of pink. The shade of lipstick was wrong too. The tips of her fingers looked unnatural, in spite of freshly painted nails. Trisha shuddered. There was no life in this imitation Christina, this cold body cradled inside the ornate casket. Trisha longed to hear someone say, *"Will the real*

Christina Eckloe please stand up?" and for her friend to jump out from behind the curtain and yell, *"Surprise!"*

"She looks beautiful, doesn't she?" Julia said, sounding as if she believed it.

"Lovely," came the answer from Trisha's mother.

Trisha couldn't utter a word. To her, there was nothing beautiful about death. Not one thing pretty about Christina in a coffin.

"Touch her if you want," Julia said, reaching out to stroke her daughter's cheek.

Trisha recoiled. She'd touched her grandmother's lifeless body years before with the curiosity of a child and had been shocked by how cold her skin had felt. In life, Grandma had been warm and soft, and had smelled faintly of lilacs. Trisha didn't want to touch this strange, icy skin of death. "No," Trisha said in answer to Julia's suggestion. "That's okay."

She sensed her dad standing behind her. She glanced to the side and saw Charlie peering at her through watery eyes. In an uncommon flash of insight, she knew he was thinking, *I'm glad this isn't you.*

"I've seen enough," she whispered, taking a step backward.

The adults flanked her all the way to the back of the room. People converged on them, and soon both sets of parents were distracted. For Trisha, it was the perfect moment to slip out of the parlor and into the larger waiting area. Once there, she felt lost. If anything, it was filled with even more people. She wanted them all to go away. She wanted to ask, *"Why are you here? She didn't even know most of you."*

Slowly, she made her way through the crowd, not finding Tucker and not sure where to go or what to do. She stopped in front of a large floral arrangement from the student body and faculty of the high school that was done up in the school's colors. Red mums on a background of yellow petals spelled Christina's name and the date she would have graduated. Emotion clogged Trisha's throat.

"I'm glad you're here," Tucker said as he came up to her. "I was hoping I wouldn't have to go in there to find you."

He wore a dark blue suit and looked more grown up, more responsible than when he was in his everyday school clothes.

"I saw her, Tucker. She looks . . . okay."

"I don't know if I can stand to look at her."

"I didn't think I could either."

"You're braver than I am—"

His sentence broke off and his eyes widened. Trisha turned around to see Christina's father hurtling toward them. He bellowed, "What are you doing here? You're a killer! You killed my daughter! Get out!"

Nine

All the color drained from Tucker's face.
"I told you to leave. Get out before I
throw you out!" Nelson Eckloe shouted.

Trisha cowered, half expecting the man to
shove her aside and strike Tucker.

All at once, her father was by her side. He
caught Nelson's arm and forced him to take a
step backward. "Stop it, Nelson. It won't help."

"I don't want him here. I don't want Julia
even to see him. He's not welcome."

Tucker looked sick. Both his parents materi-
alized on either side of him. "Now hold on,"
Tucker's father said. "You can't throw us out.
We have every right to be here."

"He killed our Christina."

Tucker tugged at his father. "Let's go. I—I don't want to cause trouble."

"You don't have to leave, son."

"Yes, I do." Tucker turned and headed straight for the door.

Trisha stood stock-still in a lobby filled with onlookers grown motionless and quiet. Tucker's father said, "It was an accident, Nelson. An *accident*. Tucker loved your daughter. You know that. They'd been together for years. He'd never have done anything to hurt her."

Christina's father pressed his lips together into a fine, harsh line, spun on his heel, and walked away. He disappeared inside the parlor. People in the lobby began to talk among themselves.

"He's distraught," Trisha's mother said to Tucker's parents. "I'm sure he didn't mean what he said."

Tucker's parents looked weary, as if they hadn't slept in days. They left the building.

"Can we please go?" Trisha asked her parents. "I need to go too."

They rode home in silence, none of them offering to discuss the events of the evening. Trisha thought a long time about what Tucker's father had said: that Tucker wouldn't have done anything to hurt Christina. It was partly true. Tucker didn't *harm* her, but he'd *hurt* her many times. With words and attitude, he'd assailed her emotions, wounded her heart, and made her cry. Tucker's love had sometimes been a burden for Christina, which was something only her closest friend knew.

Trisha sighed. Parents knew very little about what went on inside their teenagers' hearts and minds. Amazingly little.

The funeral service was held in the huge Lutheran church downtown where Christina's parents had been members all their lives. Trisha arrived early because she wanted some time alone with her thoughts and memories. The casket, already in place at the front of the church along with several of the more spectacular flower arrangements, was sealed for the service. A mantle of pale yellow roses was draped across it. Trisha plucked one perfect flower from the cascade. She would preserve it, keep it forever as a remembrance.

At the insistence of Christina's parents, she sat at the front of the church in the special pew reserved for family. Julia held her hand, sobbing intermittently. Trisha's family sat behind them, and Trisha felt comforted, knowing they were within arm's reach. The church filled for the service. Organ music washed the atmosphere in somber tones of grief. The minister paid tribute to Christina's brief life. Through it all, Trisha felt almost detached, as if she were in some movie or a dream from which she would soon awaken. It was as if her brain couldn't take it all in, nor could her soul absorb the quiet agony.

The minister posed questions about why one so young should die; yet, for all his eloquence, he had no answers. He gestured to the flowers filling the sanctuary and said something about God picking the most beautiful flowers first. Trisha thought it was rather arbitrary of God to do so. What had Tucker said to her? *God didn't play fair. But then why should he?* she thought. He was God, after all. He could do anything he wanted. And for reasons no one understood, he wanted Christina with him in heaven. Never mind the pain and anguish it caused to those left behind.

When the service was over, when the tributes had been paid, the congregation stood and six members of the high school football team, acting as pallbearers, came forward and carried the casket down the long, carpeted aisle. The pallbearers wore sunglasses, but she saw tears streaking their faces below the bottoms of the rims.

Just the summer before, she and Christina had attended a wedding in the same church. A cheerleader friend of theirs was getting married. On that day, the aisle had been strewn with rose petals, and the men in dark suits had been groomsmen. The bride, adorned in white, had all but glowed when she came down the aisle. Christina had leaned over and whispered, "This is just the way I want to get married. Tons of flowers, lots of people, and a dress to die for."

There would be no wedding for her now.

The principal had given everyone who wanted to attend Christina's funeral an excused absence from school for the morning. By the size of the funeral procession, Trisha figured the whole school had turned out. The townspeople had turned out en masse also. It had been many years since the small town had lost one of its own so tragically. "I didn't realize she was so loved," Julia said as they stood together in the cemetery watching car after car inch through the gates and down the long, winding road to the place where Christina would be laid to rest.

Julia looked dazed and, without her husband to hold her up, might have fallen over. As for Trisha, she was glad she had crutches to lean on. Using them was slow going and the undersides of her arms ached from the constant pressure, but without them, she might not have made it to the side of the grave where the casket had been carried.

Trisha shivered despite her heavy coat and gloves. Most of the previous week's snow had melted in a fickle February thaw. Sunlight poured from the sky, but it offered no warmth for all its brightness. She could hardly bear the thought of going away and leaving Christina in this cold and lonely place with nothing but stone angels to watch over her.

She wondered where Tucker was, glanced around, and saw him on the other side of the casket in a crowd of students. He wore sunglasses and a dark overcoat. If Christina's father saw him, he didn't let on. Trisha believed that Tucker had every right to be there. In spite of the accident, he'd been a part of Christina's life for many years. She longed to have Cody there too and tried not to think of him in the hospital in a coma. She vowed to remember every detail of the day so that she could tell him about it when he woke up. *If* he woke up.

The minister spoke again, read some Bible verses, then dismissed the crowd. Instead of leaving, the kids from school formed a single line, passed by the casket, and touched it. Some tossed a flower on top. Trisha felt a moment of panic. With only the rose from the mantle in her coat pocket, she had nothing to put on the casket. She felt a tug on her coat sleeve, looked down, and saw Charlie. He handed her a single white mum and stepped away. She took her place in line and tucked the flower into the mass already heaped on the casket. Tears blurred her vision. Until then, she'd been dry-eyed at the service, but this final farewell was almost more than she could bear.

"Come on, honey," her mother said, leading her away from the others.

"How can I leave her here, Mom? She was the best friend I ever had."

She went slowly back to the van, which was parked along the inner road in a long line of vehicles. She leaned against the door, looking back at the tent over the site where work-men would lower Christina's casket into the ground once the crowds were gone.

"Why don't you get out of the cold?" her dad said. "It's going to be a while before we can drive out of here. The crowd's huge."

"Not yet," Trisha said.

Someone came up to her. "Trisha? You re-member me? Harriet Kimble from the nursing home."

She looked into the nurse's kind face. "I re-member."

"I'm so sorry about Christina. This is a very sad day indeed. I read in the paper where you were hurt too. Are you doing better?"

"I'm just sore and achy."

"I'm glad. When I read about the accident, I couldn't believe it. She was just helping us out the day before, and then I read where she'd died." Tears pooled in Mrs. Kimble's soft brown eyes. "And then yesterday afternoon when the florist delivered all those flowers to the home—"

"What flowers?"

"Red carnations. Christina ordered them a

week ago. Paid for them out of her own pocket, according to the florist. Fifty-three pretty red carnations, one for every patient in the place, for us to put on their breakfast trays this morning."

Trisha's brain felt dull, her thoughts murky. "Why would she have done that?"

Mrs. Kimble's expression became surprised, then gentle. "Why, for Valentine's Day, child. Did you forget that today's Valentine's Day? She wanted everyone to have a pretty flower to brighten their day. Wasn't that just like her?"

Trisha had totally lost track of time, of the days of the week. There was something about Valentine's Day . . . something she should remember. And then all at once it came back to her: This was to have been the day Tucker asked Christina to marry him. This was to have been the day he offered her a ring, the day she might have decided to give up the scholarship to Vermont to stay in Mooresville and become his wife after graduation.

Ever since Cody had told her about Tucker's plan, Trisha had chafed against it. She had wanted her friend to take the scholarship and get away from Tucker's influence any way she could. A week ago, it had seemed so important. Today, there was to be no scholarship, no wedding, no future. Christina's span of time on earth was over.

From the distance, Trisha heard a bagpipe begin playing "Amazing Grace." The lone piper, the symbolic spirit of their school, was dressed in a Scottish kilt and tasseled cap. He stood in the sun next to the burial site, playing for Christina. The notes, haunting and melancholy, chased the wind.

"Happy Valentine's Day, Christina," Trisha whispered.

Ten

"I want to go see Cody." Trisha made her announcement as soon as she arrived home from the funeral. She'd not returned to school with the rest of the students because she couldn't bear the idea of returning to classes and going through the motions of everyday life with the pretense that things were normal again. Nothing was normal for her. Nothing.

"His mother says he's no better," her mother said.

"I don't care. I want to see him. When I was in the emergency room, you told me you'd take me to see him. You promised."

Her mother sighed. "Yes, I did. I just

thought it would be after he came out of the coma."

"Please." Trisha's voice trembled.

"All right. Let me make arrangements for Charlie to go to Darrin's house and I'll drive you in."

Trisha slept on the ride into Chicago. She didn't mean to, but exhaustion caught up with her. She hadn't slept well since the accident. At night, it took her a long time to fall asleep, and when she did, chaotic images invaded her dreams. She kept seeing flashes of the accident, pictures of the twisted car, the glittering glass broken on the snow and scattered like marbles. And something else haunted her too, images she couldn't quite get her mind around. Pictures that teased and taunted, but never came into clear focus. A blurry impression of the moments leading up to the wreck would flash in her memory, but before she could anchor it into place, it evaporated like fog. Often, the dreams woke her; her heart would be pounding and her breath would be ragged, and she'd sit straight up in bed, scared and confused and never sure why. And because she didn't want to have bad dreams again, she would turn on a light and read until it was time to begin another day.

By the time they arrived at the hospital in Chicago, it was growing dark. The vast hospital complex stretched for a city block and had an atmosphere of permanence, of solidity and strength. She was glad Cody was there and not at the small local hospital in Mooresville. This place looked serious. This place looked as if it could fix him, make him whole and well, wake him up, and send him home again.

The head trauma unit was located on the tenth floor. She rode the elevator up with her mother. They already knew his room number because Gwyn had told them what it was, but when Trisha got to the door, she almost lost the courage to go inside. She thought of all that had happened that he didn't even know about—he'd missed Chrissy's funeral and days of his life. How would he make them up? How would he feel when he knew Christina was gone forever?

Unexpectedly, Gwyn stepped into the hall and, looking surprised to see them, said, "I had no idea you'd come today."

"I couldn't help it," Trisha said. "I just

needed to see him . . . especially after this morning and the funeral and all. It's all right, isn't it?"

"Of course. That funeral was very sad."

"I didn't see you there."

"Paul and I went to the church service, but we didn't go to the graveside. Paul went on to work, and the kids are at school. My sister watches them after school so that I can spend more time here."

"Then nothing's changed for Cody?" asked Trisha's mother.

"Not yet." Gwyn looked sad.

"Can I go in?" All this time, Trisha was screwing up her courage to see her beloved Cody, comatose.

"In a minute." Gwyn studied her thoughtfully. "You should know some things first."

"What things?"

"His doctors say that although he's in a coma, there's a good chance he can hear us talking. Other patients have emerged from comas and told doctors this. Anyway, we only tell him positive things like 'We love you' and 'Please wake up'—things like that. The one thing we don't tell him is that Christina's dead. There's time enough for him to learn that after he awakens and is stronger."

"All right," Trisha said.

"Perhaps hearing your voice will be good for him. I know how much he thinks of you."

With her heart beating at trip-hammer speed, Trisha went into the room. Cody lay on the bed looking as if he were asleep. An IV hung by his bedside, and his head was wrapped in white bandages. She couldn't help making the comparison between him and Christina. In the casket, Christina had also looked as if she were sleeping. Yet she was dead. Cody lived, but in some strange, mysterious place where they couldn't reach or rouse him. He was suspended between the world of the living and the realm of the dead.

Trisha handed her crutches to her mother and leaned closer. "Hi, Cody. It's me, Trisha." She felt stupid having to introduce herself, but it seemed appropriate at the moment.

His eyelids fluttered, and her heart leaped.

"That's common," Gwyn said, crashing Trisha's hopes. "He often moans and moves, but it doesn't mean he's waking up."

Trisha continued her monologue. "Mom's here with me. And Charlie wants to come see you too. You remember Charlie, my pain-in-the-butt kid brother? You play computer games with him." Why was she talking so inanely? She loved Cody. Yet with both mothers standing by, how could she remind him of the times they'd kissed or steamed up his car windows with their breath?

"School's about the same: boring as ever," she said. "Everyone wants you to wake up and hurry back. Won't you please wake up, Cody?"

Trisha felt a tap on her shoulder. Her mother motioned for her to step aside. She took Trisha out into the hall. "You're getting worked up, honey. See? You're crying."

Trisha was shocked. She *was* crying and hadn't even known it. "It's so hard seeing him like that. I didn't know it would hurt my heart so much."

"You're wiped out. It's been a horrible few days—the accident, your injuries, Christina's death. You just went to her funeral this morning. I think you should come home, take a few days to rest, and come back on the weekend."

Trisha knew her mother was right but hated giving in. "But what if he wakes up and asks for me and I'm not here?"

Gwyn had joined them. "Your mother's

right. Go home. I'll bring you when I come on
Saturday."

Trisha felt as if they had ganged up on her,
but she was too weary, too frustrated and sad
to argue. She returned to the car with her
mother, and they rode all the way home without speaking.

Trisha returned to school on Thursday. She
didn't want to, but the principal had called to
remind her of the memorial service on Friday
and Trisha's commitment to say a few words
about Christina. She dreaded it, but what else
could she do? She had been Christina's best
friend and everybody knew it.

Tucker met her before the first bell and
asked, "Do you know what you're going to
say?"

"I wrote down some things, but no . . . I'm
still not sure."

"They didn't ask me," he said, looking dejected.

"You're lucky. I'm really dreading it."

"Maybe. It's not going to be easy to even sit
through this thing."

"At least I won't be sitting up on stage all by

myself. Three or four teachers will speak and so will the principal." She was psyching herself up and knew it.

"Yeah . . . like they really knew her." He sounded sarcastic.

"What's that supposed to mean?"

"They knew *about* her, but they didn't know her."

She had to give him credit for that. She didn't think her teachers knew Christina all that well either. Perhaps they knew the public Christina, but they surely didn't know the private one. Yet hadn't she often wondered if Tucker had ever really known and understood Christina? He never appreciated her need to go away to college or to work at the nursing home. Trisha wanted to mention it and would have if the circumstances had been different. But this wasn't the day to get into an argument with Tucker.

"I would have said something about her if they'd asked me," he said, undeterred by her silence. "They won't ask me, though, because of the accident. Because I was driving. Her parents hate me."

"That might never change."

"Our lawyer called about the inquest. The police might ask you what happened."

The news surprised and disturbed her. "I don't really remember too much," she said. "I don't know how much help I can be."

"They may wait for Cody to wake up so he can tell them what he remembers too."

"That may be a long time," she said. "I saw him after the funeral and he's pretty messed up."

"I'm going to visit him this weekend," Tucker said. "With some of the guys from the football team."

She told him what Gwyn had told her about not mentioning Christina's death, and how Cody could move but still not be awake. Suddenly she thought about the kids in the other car and asked him about them.

"They were from Henderson. They had been goofing around on the road before the wreck. Do you remember that part?"

She concentrated. "They wouldn't let us pass them. They slowed down when they got in front of us, then sped up when we tried to go around."

"That's right. Then I hit the ice and we flipped."

"Then it's sort of their fault." She kept trying to recall the exact sequence of events, but the pictures kept running together and blurring like ink on wet paper.

"I don't think so," Tucker said. "They were acting like jerks, but I slowed down just like Cody asked, so as not to egg them on. No . . . it was an accident, pure and simple."

"They did come back to help us," she said, still trying to sort out her memories. "I guess that counts for something."

"That's what the lawyer says too. If you remember anything else, will you let me know?"

"Sure." Her head was starting to hurt from the intense concentration. "I have to go to class."

"Me too. See you in the auditorium. I know you'll say the right things today about Christina. You and me, we loved her the most."

She watched him walk away, not half as confident in her ability as he was.

From her seat on the stage, Trisha watched classmates pour into the auditorium and fill up the seats. By ten-fifteen the room was packed. The students were amazingly quiet and subdued, not at all the way they were for most assemblies. An easel set to one side on the stage held a blowup of Christina's senior photograph. Trisha could hardly bear to look at it. When the bell rang, the principal stood, walked to the podium, and began to speak.

Trisha tried to concentrate on his words but couldn't. The whole scene reminded her of something from a bad movie. It didn't seem real. She kept searching the audience for Christina, even though she knew her best friend wasn't going to be there. She saw the row and the seats where they usually sat for assemblies. Two guys sat there now. *I miss you, Chrissy,* her mind kept saying.

She was startled by the sound of her name, and all at once she realized that the principal was finished and was turning the podium over to her. Trisha felt sick to her stomach. With her heart pounding, she limped to the podium. She was using only one crutch now. She heard a round of polite applause, shuffled her notes on the lectern, and cleared her throat. She looked out at the sea of faces. Every eye was on her. She glanced down at her notes and realized that the words were blurry. A tear splashed onto one of the pages.

Panicky, she looked up and opened her mouth, but nothing came out. She heard someone behind her shift in their chair. Suddenly, her shoulders started heaving and she began to cry uncontrollably. "I—I can't do this!" she sobbed.

And while everyone watched, Trisha turned and hurried off the stage, past the red velvet curtain and out the side door, into the bitter cold of the February morning.

Eleven

❦

Trisha navigated the empty hallways to a bathroom by the gym and locked herself into one of the stalls. She leaned against the cold, hard steel and cried. She cried for Christina. She cried for Cody. She cried for herself. She cried for the sheer embarrassment of breaking down in front of the entire senior class.

She was drying her eyes when she heard a tentative knock on the stall's door. "Go away," she said. "This one's occupied."

"Trisha? It's Abby Harrison. Will you open the door?"

"Abby . . . please . . . leave me alone."

"No can do. The principal sent me to find

you. I'm supposed to bring you to the office. Actually, I volunteered," Abby added when Trisha didn't answer.

"And why would you do that?"

"Because I know what you've been going through."

Trisha unlocked the door, threw it open, and glared at Abby. "People say that all the time. But it's a lie! Nobody knows how I feel. How could you?"

Abby stepped aside as Trisha brushed past her and crossed to the row of sinks. She tagged after Trisha and stood beside her while Trisha washed her face with cool water. Abby said, "I know because when I was in middle school, my older brother, Carson, fell asleep at the wheel of his car, crashed into a telephone pole, and died."

Trisha looked up, catching Abby's brown-eyed gaze in the mirror.

Abby held her gaze. "It was the worst year of my life. Everything reminded me of him. At home his room was next to mine. I couldn't pass the door without breaking down."

"I'm sorry. I didn't know."

"And don't forget the year of 'firsts' ahead of you—things you have to get through without her. First birthday—yours and hers. First

Christmas. First day of school. First anniversary of her death. Well, you get the picture."

Trisha got it. "If you're trying to make me feel worse—"

"No way. I just want you to know, you're not the first person to have this happen. Friends and people we love die. It's horrible. But you don't have to go through it alone."

"I lost it in front of the whole class. I was supposed to say wonderful things about her, and when the time came, I lost it. I let her down. I let her memory down."

"No one thinks any less of you. Everyone knew it was going to be hard for you to stand up there and say a bunch of stuff when you're still so broken up. The principal knows it too, and if you'll come to the office with me, he and Mrs. Dodge are going to apologize for putting you on the spot that way. They realize they made a mistake."

Trisha blotted her face on paper towels. Her reflection in the mirror looked ghastly. Her lip was still puffy, and the bruising under her eye had turned an ugly yellowish blue. "I don't need his apology. I just want to go home."

"He feels guilty. If we ask real nice, I'm sure he'll let me drive you home."

"Do you think so?"

"Let's ask." Abby retrieved Trisha's crutch and gave it to her.

Trisha got to the door, stopped, and turned.

"What's wrong?" Abby asked.

"I used be the one who went to find Christina when she was hiding and crying in the bathroom. It was one of my roles in her life."

"Did she do it often?"

"More and more this year. And it was always about Tucker Hanson. They were supposed to be in love, but he made her pretty unhappy at times."

Abby pulled open the door for Trisha. "Well, I promise not to chase you down whenever you want to hide in the bathroom and cry. Just come find me when you feel that way, and we'll talk." She flipped her hair off her shoulder. "I really do know how bad you hurt, Trisha. I really, really do."

The principal was generous to Trisha and allowed Abby to take her home. Her mother met them at the door and, after thanking Abby, ushered Trisha into the kitchen. "Why didn't you tell me you were asked to speak at

the memorial service?" she asked. "I certainly
would have advised you against it."

Trisha shrugged listlessly. "It seemed like the
right thing to do at the time. I didn't expect to
get blindsided by my own emotions. I wanted
to pay tribute to her, Mom. All I did was make
a fool of myself."

"I can't imagine anyone at school thinking
that. And if they do, then they're made of
stone." Trisha's mother fixed a cup of hot tea
and set it in front of her. "Do you know what
today is?" she asked.

Trisha shook her head.

"It's Friday. You're supposed to have your
stitches removed today."

"The accident happened a week ago," Trisha
said. She remembered Abby's words: "a year of
firsts." This was the end of the first week since
Christina had died.

"And you'll never have to go through this
week again. It's behind you. You made it
through."

Yes, she had, but at the moment, it was cold
comfort.

"Tell you what," her mother said, picking
up the phone. "I'm going to call and see if I

can't move your appointment up, and if I can, afterward I'll take you into Charlene's for a total makeover. New haircut, manicure, the works. What do you say?"

Trisha didn't think much of the idea, but her mother was trying so hard to cheer her up that she knew she couldn't refuse her offer. "Fine," she said with little enthusiasm.

Their family doctor checked Trisha over and removed the stitches in her head. "You look good," he said. "The knee's going to take some more pampering, but considering what your body's been through, you're doing amazingly well."

Better than Cody, she thought. "So when can I lose the crutch?"

"When you can put weight on the leg without your knee hurting, you can chuck it. Maybe in a week or so." He peered at her over the tops of his glasses, his expression turning fatherly. "And the next time you get in a car with your friends, put your seat belt on."

The hair salon, Charlene's, made a fuss over Trisha when she arrived. The stylist set to work giving her a trendy cut to cover the shaved spot on her head. "I was letting it grow long," Trisha said while the stylist snipped and trimmed.

"By this summer, it'll be long again. It's hair. Hair grows." The woman flashed a smile in the mirror where Trisha watched her transformation. She thought of all the times she and Christina had pored through magazines studying hairstyles, laughing and experimenting with gels, creams, and temporary color. She remembered the time Christina put a blond rinse in her hair, which turned it pink. "*I look like a troll*," Christina had wailed. Trisha had come to her rescue by helping her recolor it brown, though it took many weeks to finally return to its natural shade of honey blond.

Trisha's mother spared no expense, and by the time they left the salon, Trisha's hair looked perfect, her nails were buffed and trimmed, and she had a new concealer that artfully hid the bruising under her eye and along her cheek. She felt better too.

Around five, they pulled into the driveway. Her mother had no sooner turned off the engine than Charlie came running out the front door. "Boy, am I glad you're home!" he shouted. His cheeks were flushed and he looked ready to explode.

"Slow down. What's wrong?" asked Trisha's mother.

"Nothing's wrong!" He grabbed Trisha's arm. "Cody's mother called. Cody woke up."

Gwyn's message had been on the answering machine when Charlie got home from school, he said. Trisha and her mother didn't even stop to call the hospital, they just got in the car and headed into Chicago. If the car could have sprouted wings, it wouldn't have gotten to the hospital fast enough to suit Trisha. Once there, she hurried to the elevator and, with her heart pounding, rode it to the tenth floor.

Just as she came down the hall, she saw Gwyn step out of Cody's room. Heedless of the hospital's rules about silence, she called, "Mrs. McGuire! How is he? Charlie said Cody's awake."

Gwyn looked tired, but she was smiling. "He opened his eyes around noon. I was sitting next to his bed and reading. He just said, 'Hi,' clear as you please."

By now Trisha's mother, who had parked the car after leaving Trisha at the entrance, had caught up with Trisha. "We're so happy to hear the good news about Cody," she said with a beaming smile.

"Can I go in?" Trisha asked.

"You should know some things first," Gwyn said, her expression growing serious. "He's different—not quite himself yet."

"That's okay. He's been through a lot. I won't stay long." Trisha recalled how hard it had been for her to concentrate during the past week. She understood that Cody might be having problems too.

She started inside the room. Gwyn caught her arm. "We should talk. His memory—"

"Please, can we talk later? All I want right now is to see him." Trisha had grown increasingly impatient. She didn't want to stand in the hall discussing Cody. She wanted to throw her arms around his neck and tell him how happy she was that he was awake. She wanted to tell him how much she'd missed him and how scared she'd been for his life.

Trisha eased out of Gwyn's hold and went into the room. The top half of the mechanical bed had been raised and Cody was sitting up, eating a dish of ice cream. "Cody!" she cried. Moisture filled her eyes, and for the first time in days, she shed tears of joy.

He looked startled. She wished he didn't have to see her with a crutch. "Hi," she said, reaching out to touch him.

He drew back, his eyes wary, clouded, an expression of bewilderment on his face. "I'm sorry," he said, his voice almost a monotone. "Do I know you?"

Twelve

"Cody, don't kid around. It's not funny," Trisha said. She propped her crutch against the wall and opened her arms. "Don't you know how worried I've been about you?"

He looked past her. "Mom? Mother?"

Gwyn was by his side instantly. "Cody, this is Trisha. She's a friend from school." Her voice sounded soft, soothing, as if she were explaining something complex to a frightened child. She warned Trisha with her gaze to play along.

"I—I don't remember." Cody looked more confused.

The implications of the situation hit Trisha hard and fast. The coma had affected his memory.

Cody looked back at Trisha shyly. "I'm sorry. I don't mean to . . ." His sentence trailed off as if he'd lost interest in it. Once again his voice didn't sound normal to her.

Trisha took a step backward. "It's all right. I shouldn't have barged in on you."

She got out of the room as fast as she could and leaned into the wall in the corridor for support, numb with shock. "What happened?" her mother asked.

"He didn't know me."

"What? How can that be?"

Gwyn appeared. "That's what I was trying to tell you before you went into the room. The coma's left Cody with some amnesia. His doctor says memory loss happens sometimes. Usually it's temporary. His brain's had a terrible trauma, and it may take some time before he's completely himself again."

"Does he remember anything?" Trisha's mother asked.

"He thinks he's still in middle school."

"But that was *years* ago," Trisha said. No wonder he didn't remember her. They'd only started dating in high school.

"But he *will* improve," Trisha's mother said hopefully.

"We hope so." Gwyn wrung her hands. "But there's also the possibility that he'll experience some personality changes."

"Meaning?" Trisha asked.

"We don't know yet. We just have to take it one day at a time."

"And his voice?"

"Yes. I know it sounds like a monotone. That's also a side effect of the coma. However, his doctor says he'll begin to sound more normal as he hears others talk. Just like a baby learns to imitate by hearing others."

Trisha was reeling from what she was hearing. "So I guess you don't have to worry about telling him about Christina. He doesn't even know she existed."

"Not yet, but I'm sure he'll remember eventually."

"What if he doesn't? What if he never remembers her, or me, or anything about high school?"

"We're not thinking that way, Trisha. And I don't want you thinking that way either. He *will* come back to us. I know he will."

Trisha could only stare at the floor. Her heart felt pulverized, her emotions tattered.

An already terrible day had just gotten worse—her Cody, the love of her life, didn't even remember who she was or what they'd meant to each other. And there were no guarantees that he ever would.

Trisha slept fitfully and called Abby first thing Saturday morning.

"I'll be right over," Abby told her on the phone.

When Abby arrived, Trisha pulled her into her room and told her everything that had happened with Cody. She was crying by the time she finished her story.

"Low blow," Abby said, patting Trisha on the back and handing her a wad of tissue.

"I feel like my whole life's falling apart. Two of the most important people in my life are gone—one's dead and the other doesn't know me."

"That can change," Abby said. "Cody will get his memory back, in time. I mean, once he comes home and friends drop by to visit him, he'll start to remember."

"How can you be so sure?"

"It's logical. Right now, he's in a strange

place, a hospital far from home. Once he gets home, in his room, around all the things he's grown up with, it will jog his memory. Just you wait and see."

"Do you think?" What Abby was saying made sense, and it was the first ray of hope Trisha had seen since the hospital visit.

"I'm no doctor, but I'll bet you anything, things will come back to him when he's in his own space."

"I don't know . . . If you could have seen the look on his face yesterday when he saw me. No recognition. None. *Nada*. Zilch. I was a total stranger." Her hope spiraled downward as she recalled Cody's expression of befuddlement and panic when she'd tried to hug him. "This is a nightmare, Abby— A real nightmare."

"I know it seems that way now, but—"

"It *is* that way. I couldn't even get through a simple memorial service for Christina, and Cody may never remember her or me. Can it get any worse?"

"Cody's alive and he's expected to recover. As I see it, that's a big plus."

Trisha wandered over to her desk and to the

bulletin board hanging above it. It was filled with snapshots of her and Cody and her and Christina from happier times. "If I take these down, the board will be blank," she said sadly. "These two people filled up my life, but now . . ."

"Don't take them down. They're good memories. I still have pictures of Carson in my scrapbooks and on my bedside table. I'll never remove them."

"I feel like I should be doing more to keep Christina's memory alive."

Abby studied her. "Is that what you're afraid of? That she'll be forgotten?"

Trisha nodded.

"Get your coat. I want to take you somewhere."

In Abby's car, Trisha leaned her head back against the seat and shut her eyes, trying to gather her composure. Was this how it was going to be from now on? Was she going to fall apart every single day for the rest of her life?

The car slowed, pulled over, and stopped. Trisha sat up and looked out the window. She saw a field, patchy with snow. She didn't have to ask where they were. She knew.

"Come on," Abby said, getting out of the car. "I want you to see something."

Trisha followed. The field was scarred by the impact of the accident that had changed so many lives so quickly. A stick held a tattered piece of material; it fluttered in the chilly breeze. Tucker's car had been towed away, but large gouges were ripped in the earth and a few glittering pieces of glass caught the sunlight, reminding Trisha of what had happened there. She felt as desolate and windswept as the field looked. She shivered.

"This is what I brought you to see," Abby said.

Trisha turned and her breath caught. In the ditch was a lone white cross made of sticks held together by a strip of rawhide. Hundreds of flowers adorned the area, stretching for yards up and down the ditch. "It's for Christina," Abby said. "Kids from school, kids from Henderson, people from all over the area have been coming here all week and leaving flowers and stuff."

Trisha walked to the makeshift memorial, bent, and retrieved a folded scrap of paper that was tucked into a cluster of flowers tied with a ribbon. She unfolded it, read, "We miss you," and saw that it was signed by four girls she did not know. She refolded the paper and tucked it back into the flowers. She read another note, and another, and another, careful not to crush any of the flowers heaped on the ground. Many of the bouquets were dead or frozen, but many were fresh, as if they'd just been dropped off.

Abby put her arm around Trisha's waist. "See? No one's going to forget Christina. Before the spring rains come, we're going to move the cross up to the shoulder of the road for everyone who drives past to see. The cheerleaders from her squad have already made sure flowers will be put out here once a week until school's over for the year.

"People care, Trisha . . . a lot of them cared about Christina. We all lost her. In a way, we all lost part of ourselves the night she died."

Tears had frozen on Trisha's cheeks. She stood with Abby while five years of memories washed over her. She had thought she'd have a lifetime of friendship with Christina, but her best friend was dead. Everything was different now.

"You had breakfast?" Abby asked, her voice sounding cheerful.

"Not yet."

"Me either. Let's go chow down on pancakes at Millie's." That was a popular local restaurant. "My treat."

Trisha returned to the car and took one long, lingering look back at the roadside memorial. It occurred to her that the town cemetery held Christina's body, but her memory would be held here in the shape of a small, handmade white cross, planted next to a cornfield on the side of a country road in northern Indiana.

Trisha really didn't want to go back to school on Monday, but her parents insisted. "You have to pick up the pieces and go on," her father told her. "I know you've been through a terrible ordeal, but you still have to go on."

"It's your senior year," her mother added. "You need to look ahead and think about graduation and college in the fall. Life goes on, honey."

Trisha certainly didn't feel like going on. She felt confused and aimless, like a swimmer treading water or a car stuck in neutral, unable to go backward, unwilling to go forward. If it hadn't been for Abby's friendship and sympathetic ear, Trisha was sure she would have gone crazy.

"Is it true about Cody?" Tucker asked her when he saw her at her locker on Monday.

"It's true."

"I was supposed to visit him on Saturday, but when I called, his mother said not to come. She told me what had happened when you went."

"Maybe he'll improve when he gets home to his room and his personal stuff." Trisha used Abby's line of reasoning because Tucker looked pretty upset. After all, he and Cody had been friends.

"His mom told me she's bringing him home today."

The news jolted her. She felt her face flush because she hadn't known, and if she really cared about him, then she *should* have known. She should have called to check on him, but hadn't because she'd been too afraid of facing rejection again.

Tucker added, "His mom said that he's improving and that his doctors can't do anything more, so they think he should come home and pick up where he left off."

Trisha slammed her locker hard enough to make kids turn around and look her way. "That's so stupid! How are any of us supposed to pick up where we left off? It can't be done, Tucker."

"Don't I know it. I can't tell you how much I miss Christina. Every minute I'm awake, I think of her. I mean, I talked to that girl practically every day of my life." He shifted his weight, leaning his shoulder into the bank of lockers. "I have her voice on my answering machine at home. She called me the day of the basketball game to tell me she loved me. I'm never going to erase that tape."

Trisha realized that as bad as things were for her, they must be worse for Tucker. She wasn't sure whom he had to talk to about it. "She really did love you, Tucker." It was useless to bring up the past and her list of gripes about the way he treated Christina. Those days were over for good. He could never hurt Christina's feelings again.

"Don't give up on Cody," he said.

She saw moisture pooling in his eyes, and she felt ashamed of her self-pity. "I don't want to give up. But how can I have something special with somebody who doesn't even remember who I am?"

A bitter smile crossed Tucker's face. "At least he's alive, Trisha. At least you can talk to him. Go *make* him remember you."

Thirteen

❧

Trisha gathered her courage, called Cody's house after school on Tuesday, and talked to his mother. "He sleeps a lot," Gwyn told her. "But he seems comfortable in his room. I know he remembers the house, but frankly he doesn't talk that much."

"He never was a big talker," Trisha said, offering encouragement.

"That's true. We're just so glad to have him home again that I'm trying to overlook the negatives. He'll be seeing a specialist in head trauma recovery, and we're hoping the specialist can help bring Cody all the way back."

"Um, I'd really like to come visit him. I don't want to freak him out like last time, but

I thought maybe, if we can talk, it might help his memory."

"A few of his old friends have called—Tucker Hanson for one, but I've not let anyone come yet. I think he needs more time."

"Sure. I understand." Trisha couldn't hide her disappointment.

"Oh, what the heck," Gwyn said quickly. "Come by tomorrow after school. That'll give me time to prepare him for your visit. I know this is difficult for you, Trisha, because you and Cody have been so close. I'm not trying to be cruel."

"No, it's okay. Really. I'll come over about four. And I won't stay long."

She hung up, feeling both scared and elated.

Gwyn met Trisha at the front door and gave her a warm, encouraging smile. "He's in his room. I told him you were coming and that you were going to tell him about school. He tries hard to remember details and gets frustrated when he can't, so if you see it starting to happen, move on to something else. Fortunately, I guess, he's easily distracted."

Trisha headed up the stairs, a sense of the familiar overcoming her. She and Cody had spent so many afternoons studying in his room or downstairs in the den. It was hard to believe that he didn't remember it as she did. She knocked on his partially open bedroom door.

He invited her in. She pasted on a smile and peeked into the space she knew so well. He was sitting in a chair at his desk, papers and photographs spread across the top. "You're Trisha," he said. "Mom said you'd come."

"And here I am." She dragged another chair to the desk and sat, careful not to infringe on his personal space. She didn't want to make him feel uncomfortable.

"I'm sorry I went nutsy on you at the hospital."

"Not a problem. I should have listened more closely to what your mother was saying about your amnesia." She was glad to hear that his voice sounded normal again.

He stared at her with such open curiosity for such a long time that she began to squirm. She kept reminding herself that although this was Cody, it wasn't *her* Cody. The face and body looked the same, but the mind was damaged, the memories fragmented.

"We knew each other," he said, picking up a picture of the two of them in his living room, hugging and mugging for the camera in front of last year's Christmas tree. "We liked each other." These were statements, not questions.

"You could say that. We liked each other a lot."

He nodded. "You're in a lot of my pictures." He picked up several and fanned them out for her to see. They were younger in some of the photos, while others had been taken only weeks before. "Did I know you for a long time?"

"A couple of years. We started dating when we were sophomores."

He hung his head. "I don't remember."

"It's all right," she said quickly. "The good news is that I can tell you how wonderful I am and you'll believe me."

The old Cody would have laughed, made some smart remark. This Cody simply stared. Finally a half-smile crept across his face. "You're teasing me."

"A little." She picked up a photo of them at the Christmas dance. "We had an interesting time this night. You picked me up, and on the way we got a flat tire and—"

"Stop." He looked upset and pressed his palms against his temples. "It hurts my head when I try to remember and can't."

She tossed the photo down quickly. "Sorry." By now, she felt jumpy and nervous. She couldn't even carry on a conversation with this Cody. He was a stranger.

"I'm not mad at you," he said, his voice halting. "I don't mean to sound angry."

What had Gwyn suggested? *Distract him. Change the subject.* "Why don't you tell me what you do remember? Maybe I can fill in the blanks for you."

"There're so many blanks. It's like trying to put together a puzzle but without knowing what the finished picture's supposed to look like." His brow puckered. "I see things in my head but they don't make sense to me."

"It's the same for me. But my senseless pictures are from the night of the accident."

"Were you hurt badly?" he asked.

"Cuts and bruises mostly. I wobbled around on crutches for a while, but I'm finished with them now. I was lucky."

"Mom told me about the accident. It's funny that I can't remember any of it, especially when it's made so much difference in my life." He looked sad. "I don't remember it at all. When I close my eyes, I see . . ." He paused. "I see a pretty girl, but she isn't you."

Trisha fished through the photos. "This girl?"

"Yes. Mom told me she died in the wreck."

He said it without emotion, which cut Trisha to the quick. "She was our friend. Her name is—was—Christina. We were on a double date that night."

"That's what Mom said."

"What do you remember?"

"Now? I remember words, but not always in the order they're supposed to go."

"What about the past?"

"Coming home from school and playing Nintendo. I remember that really clearly. But Mom says that I haven't played Nintendo since ninth grade. Next I remember waking up in the hospital. Everything in between is jumbled. The pictures flash in my head once in a while, but I can't hang on to them. They fade."

She felt discouraged. He had such a long way to go. "What about school? You've taken a lot of classes and tons of tests over the years. Will you have to start all over again?"

"I remember some of the stuff I learned in school. Mom says I'll have to take some tests in a few weeks to see where I am. I just hope I can catch up if I'm really far behind."

"You were pretty good in math." She had an

idea. Reaching for a pencil, she scribbled out an algebra problem.

He pondered it, took the pencil, and solved it.

She clapped. "That's great! See? You haven't forgotten everything."

He looked at her, grinning sheepishly. "I don't know how I did it, though. Or if I can do it again."

"Your memory's going to come back, Cody. I'll help you. All our friends will help." She took the pencil and wrote down her phone number. "Call me any time you want."

He studied the piece of paper, then said the numbers aloud. "I probably knew this by heart, didn't I?"

"And you will again." She could tell he was tired, so she stood and told him she had to go. She didn't want to leave him. She wanted to sit in his lap and cuddle in his arms. She wanted to kiss him.

He didn't try to touch her. He just leaned back in his chair and looked her full in the face. "If you were my girlfriend, it shows I have good taste," he said.

The compliment touched her. "Thank you." She bowed slightly and he smiled fully. And for that moment, he was the Cody from her past. That gave her more hope than she'd known since before the accident.

The next day, during a yearbook work session, Trisha told Abby and Frank about her afternoon with Cody. The final drafts were supposed to be turned in by mid-April so that the school could have finished books by June. Trisha knew she hadn't been pulling her weight as an editor, but the project had lost all importance to her. "He's Cody, but he's not Cody," she said, finishing up her story. "It's hard to explain."

"When is he coming back to school?" Abby asked.

"Not for a while. His mother said she's getting a home school teacher to help him. He has trouble concentrating. She doesn't think he could sit still in classes all day either."

"Hey, neither can I," Frank said. "Maybe I can go over and get tutored with him."

Abby slugged him in the arm. "Be serious."

"I am."

Trisha ignored their interruption. "He still sleeps a lot. It's his brain's way of healing itself, according to his mother. Right now, he needs time."

"Problem is," Abby said, "graduation is less than four months away. Can he catch up?"

"I don't know. It's depressing. Here he's gone through twelve years of school and now he has to stop and play catch-up. All because of the accident." Trisha rested her chin on her palm. "I never dreamed our senior year would turn out this way. I thought it was going to be perfect."

Frank glanced at Abby. "We want to show you something that we hope will perk you up." He got up, went to a stack of large manila envelopes, brought them back to the table, extracted pictures, and spread them out. "Abby and I worked on this for days with Mrs. Krebs." She was the teacher overseeing production of the yearbook. "It's a special two-page spread in the senior section honoring Christina. What do you think?"

Trisha gazed at candid and formal shots of her friend that spanned three years of high school. Christina hanging crepe paper in the gym for the junior dance. Christina wearing mismatched and garish clothes for senior dress-down day. Christina painting a mural on the senior wall next to the school office. Trisha and Christina singing a duet for choral competition as sophomores—they'd taken a "superior" in the contest. Christina and Tucker in the Homecoming Court. The memorial floral arrangement the student body and faculty had sent to Christina's service.

"The pages will have a thick black border around them and a banner that says 'In Memoriam'," Abby added.

Emotion closed Trisha's throat. Christina's high school days had been reduced to a couple of pages that held such finality. It was a tribute to the past, to what *was*, to unrealized potential, to unfulfilled dreams. She cleared her throat. She couldn't break down like this every time someone touched the wound on her heart. "It's very nice," she said.

"We thought that if there's something special you'd like to add . . ." Frank let his sentence drift.

"No," Trisha said. "You've done a good job. There's nothing I can add."

"If you change your mind, this section doesn't go to the press until tomorrow."

"The pages are fine. Just fine."

Trisha was setting the table for dinner that evening when the doorbell rang. "Can you get it?" her mother asked. "My hands are full."

Trisha went to the door and found a policeman dressed in a gray uniform standing on the porch. "I'm Officer Harry Doyal of the Indiana Highway Patrol," he said. "I'm looking for Trisha Thompson. I'm here to ask some questions about the night Christina Eckloe died."

Fourteen

❧

"**I**'m filing my final report," Officer Doyal told Trisha and her mother once they were all settled in the living room. He pulled out a small tablet and a stubby pencil.

"What do you need to know?" Trisha's mother asked. "My daughter was injured, but she was only a passenger in the car."

"I'm just gathering information for the coroner's inquest. Whenever someone dies on the road, we have to investigate all aspects of the accident." He turned to Trisha. "Can you tell me what you remember about that night?"

"Not too much. We were headed to the Pizza Hut and the car went off the road. We ended up in a field. I was thrown out of the car and I was unconscious, but I don't know for how long." Elusive images still haunted her about the accident, but she couldn't grab hold of them. She thought it best not to discuss what she couldn't remember. The police only wanted the facts.

"What do you recall about the weather conditions?"

"It was cold but clear."

"Any ice?"

"The road looked like it had been salted. But Tucker said he hit ice, so I guess there must have been some."

"It could have been black ice," her mother suggested, using the term for invisible slick spots of frozen oily film.

"Any moonlight?" the officer asked.

"Yes."

Her mother interrupted. "Can't you get that information from other sources?"

"Of course. However, I'm interested in Trisha's perceptions of that night." Officer Doyal turned back to Trisha and asked, "Would you say that Mr. Hanson was driving safely?"

She thought hard before answering. "I—I think so. We were going fast—"

"Too fast?"

"I couldn't see the speedometer. I was sitting behind the driver's seat so that I could talk more easily to my friend Christina in the front passenger seat." She had a clear picture of Christina from the back. The console, with the gearshift, was between Christina and Tucker. Trisha had a sudden image of Tucker downshifting. "Cody, my boyfriend, asked Tucker to slow down and he did," Trisha said.

"Why did Cody ask him to slow down? Do you remember?"

"There was another car full of guys that pulled alongside of us. They started horsing around, going past us and slowing down, then speeding up if we tried to pass them."

"So this other car was giving Mr. Hanson a hard time?"

"Sort of. But we were ignoring them."

"And then what happened?"

Trisha concentrated on getting a clearer picture of the moments before the accident. "I . . . don't . . . know. All of a sudden we were skidding, and then things went dark for me. I'm sorry, I can't remember any more." She felt as if she'd somehow failed Christina. "Maybe the guys in the other car saw more of what happened."

"I've already interviewed them. Their story's pretty much the same."

"Perhaps Cody can tell you more," Trisha's mother said.

"I've already talked to Mr. McGuire, but his parents insist that his head injury prevents him from remembering the accident at all."

"That's true," Trisha said, anxious to protect Cody. "He's been in a coma and can't remember the past few years, much less the night of the accident."

"Have you talked to Tucker yet?" Trisha's mother asked.

"He's next," Officer Doyal said.

"And then what will happen?" Trisha asked.

"I'll file my report and a judge will review it. If he thinks there was any neglect on the driver's part, he'll rule the accident a vehicular homicide."

Trisha gulped. "You mean Tucker could go to jail?"

"That depends on a lot of other factors—his driving record, his character, his testimony.

The judge has plenty of leeway, and Tucker's family has a good attorney."

"But Trisha won't be asked to testify, will he?" her mother asked. "I mean, you heard her say so yourself: she doesn't remember any details."

"That's up to the judge, ma'am."

"How long before we know anything?"

"That depends on how crowded the court docket is and how soon we can get everything in place for a hearing." The officer fished out a business card and stood. "If you think of anything else, please call me. You take care, Trisha. I'm sorry about your friend. I understand she was a fine girl."

Trisha nodded; then her mother walked with Officer Doyal to the door.

Trisha remained on the sofa, feeling numb. She kept remembering the conversations she'd had with Tucker about the accident. He had asked her questions. What had she told him? Had he been trying to find out what she remembered so that he could vent and grieve? Or did he have a different motive? One that included protecting himself?

She shook her head, unable and unwilling

to dwell on that idea. Tucker had love
Christina. If he was one bit responsible fo
her death, he'd admit it . . . wouldn't he? I
only she could remember more details. *I
only*.

"If he's got nothing to hide, why doe
Tucker need a lawyer?" This was Trisha's firs
question to Abby when she found her at he
locker before school the next morning.

"Standard procedure," Abby said. "And be
sides, Tucker told you his family had a lawye
already."

"I know, but after talking to the cop, I
started to wonder about it. Maybe he's cover
ing up something."

"I'm sure it's routine, Trisha. My dad ever
got a lawyer when Carson died and there
wasn't any other car involved. But he wante
to make sure that the car was in working or
der—it had been in the shop just the week be
fore. He wanted a lawyer to represent Carson'
best interests, because we were so devastate
we couldn't think straight." She spun the dia
on her combination lock. "As it turned out, the
autopsy proved that he'd fallen asleep at th
wheel. I don't know how they can be so sur

of that, but they were. So the accident was just an accident."

"I keep thinking I'm not remembering everything, like if I can just get a handle on these pictures that keep flashing through my mind, I'll know exactly what happened. It's making me crazy."

"Don't be so down on yourself. It's hard, because you really want to blame somebody for it and there may be nobody to blame."

"It isn't fair. We got into Tucker's car that night to come home from a basketball game. The accident should never have happened."

"Hey, don't be upset." Abby reached over and squeezed Trisha's hand. "Of course it isn't fair. But don't beat yourself up trying to figure out why it happened. Just accept that it happened and there was nothing you could have done to stop it."

"I hope that's true."

"Bad things happen," Abby said, "and sometimes it's nobody's fault. When I was going through losing Carson, my mantra became a quote I read in a card somebody sent. It was: 'That which doesn't kill us, makes us stronger.' You may not believe it now, Trisha, but this will make you stronger too."

"But a whole lot sadder," Trisha added. "Oh, Abby, so much sadder."

On Saturday, with Gwyn's permission, Trisha visited Cody again. The March day had turned springlike, with temperatures in the fifties. Sunshine shimmered through still-bare tree branches. She and Cody found a spot on the back deck of his house, sheltered from any chilling breezes by a short brick wall. They lifted their faces toward the warming rays of the sun.

"They say this is bad for us," Trisha commented. "That the sun causes skin cancer."

"I don't care. It feels good, and I'm going stir-crazy being stuck inside the house all the time."

"I don't care either." At the moment, cancer didn't seem like half the threat that everyday life did. She asked, "Did you know that spring break's in a few weeks? Some of the seniors' parents have rented a bus to take a group to Florida. Everyone has to pay their own way, but there's a nice place to stay right on the beach."

"Are you going?"

If Christina had been alive, they would probably all have been going. "No," Trisha said.

"Do you want to go?"

Not without you, she thought. "It wouldn't be much fun for me."

"I'd like to go somewhere . . . anywhere. But Mom won't let me out of her sight."

Trisha knew from talking to Gwyn that Cody was still not in any shape to go anywhere. He got confused easily and lost his temper frequently. His comeback was slow, taking longer than she had ever imagined. "How's the tutoring going?" she asked.

"All right some days. Not so good others. Sometimes I read a page in a book and it makes perfect sense. Other times, it's gibberish. I lost it the other day and threw the book across the room. The tutor wasn't real happy about that." He glanced over at her. "How's real school?"

"I feel like I'm wandering the halls and filling up chairs in classes. I really don't care about it anymore."

"But you have to care. Your head's fine."

She smiled ruefully. "You think so? Some days I'm not so sure."

He looked puzzled, then smiled. "You're joking again."

"Just a little." She felt sad around him, as if he was missing in action and someone had sent an impostor to take his place. Yet she couldn't give up on him. It wouldn't be right to abandon him just because he was different now. Just because he couldn't remember their past together and all they'd meant to each other.

"Could I ask you a favor?"

She started, realizing that her thoughts had wandered and that he was looking at her searchingly. "Sure," she said.

"Could I . . . Would you mind if I touched your face?"

"Why?"

"My doctor says that sometimes fingers have memories even when the head doesn't. He said that touching can trigger things for some patients. I want to touch you, Trisha, because I want to remember you from before."

Her heart began to thud. "It's okay with me." She leaned forward and he very carefully stroked her cheek, then her hair. Shivers shot up her spine. It had been so long since Cody had touched her, really touched her, that her skin was starving for him. "We used to play a game sometimes," she said. "You'd come up behind me in the hall and ask, 'Who loves you, babe?' and I'd say, 'Have we met?' and you'd say, 'Don't tell me you're spoken for. Am I going to have to take some guy out before we can live happily ever after?' And I'd say, 'No. You're the one I want.' And you'd say—"

"Forever." Cody interrupted her.

"Yes, yes. You'd say, 'Forever,' and I'd say 'Forever' back to you. Do you remember that?" She felt her heart beating really hard and searched his eyes for some light of recognition.

"Not all of it. But the word was there for me. I knew what word to say, didn't I?"

"You knew." Her vision blurred as tears welled in her eyes.

He grinned and dipped his forehead so that it touched hers, and together they sat in the heat of the sun, their fingers intertwined, holding on to the sweet moment of victory.

Trisha returned home, fairly bursting to tell someone her news. Her mother rushed out of the kitchen waving an envelope, her face beaming. "Look what came for you today in the mail," she said. "It's from the admissions office of Indiana University, Trisha. It's a big fat envelope filled with paperwork. I'm certain it's your acceptance for fall classes. Oh, honey! Open it right away."

Fifteen

"College?" The news had come so far out of left field that Trisha felt off balance, as if she'd been shoved and couldn't regain her footing.

"Yes, college. Remember all those forms we filled out last fall? Well, here's the payoff for twelve hard years of schoolwork." She shoved the envelope into Trisha's hands. "Come on, open it. The suspense is killing me."

Trisha's fingers trembled, but not from excitement or expectation. She tore open the envelope and pulled out a sheaf of papers. Her mother stood beside her, peering over Trisha's shoulder. The letter began, "*Congratulations. You've been accepted for fall semester. . . .*"

Her mother clapped and hugged her. "I knew it! I was right! Oh, honey, congratulations! I'm so proud of you."

Trisha thrust the envelope at her mother, took a backward step. "Mom . . . I don't know what to say."

"Say 'Thank you, the check's in the mail.' Wait until your dad sees this. He's going to be so pleased." Trisha's mother glanced at Trisha and must have noticed that Trisha wasn't jumping up and down the way she was. "What's wrong? I thought you'd be thrilled. We've been planning this for years."

"*You've* been planning this for years," Trisha corrected.

"But you've always worked hard for grades good enough to attend college. We've discussed it for years. Saved for it for years."

"So much has changed now."

"What?" Her mother looked genuinely bewildered.

"How can you ask that? My best friend's dead. My boyfriend, who was planning on going to IU with me, probably won't be able to go at all. Everything's changed."

"Trisha, the accident's behind you. September is months away. You'll feel differently when all your other friends are packing up to go off to college. You've got to start focusing on your future."

Trisha threw up her hands in frustration. "Get a clue, Mom! I can't handle the future right now. Don't you understand? Why can't you understand?"

Trisha spun and ran toward the stairs, her mother's voice calling her name, chasing her up the stairs with its shrillness. She slammed her bedroom door, flung herself across the bed, and cried harder than she had since Christina's funeral.

Trisha didn't come down for supper. She remained in her room, sitting in the dark. Her father came up to her room eventually and sat down next to her on the bed. "How are you, honey? Can we talk?" he asked.

"I'm sure Mom's told you that I'm horrible. And that I'm an ungrateful brat."

"No. She's worried about you. I'm worried about you."

"Well, don't be." Trisha hunkered down against the headboard, holding a pillow against her chest as if it offered some defense.

"Look, we all know that these past weeks

have been hell for you. No one is trying to ignore what happened. It hasn't been easy on any of us."

It seemed like a strange thing for him to say. To her way of thinking, life had gone on quite normally in their household. "I know I've not been myself—"

"Honey, the accident isn't just about you. It's involved all of us." He sat silent for a minute, then finally asked, "Remember the time you fell off your bike and skinned the whole side of your leg?"

"You kicked the bike and bent it."

"I was so mad at that stupid bike for allowing you to get hurt."

Even at the time she'd thought his anger was irrational, but it had made her feel good to see him get even with the thing that had hurt her. "You put medicine on my leg and took me out for ice cream. Then you had to come home and fix my bike."

"I couldn't stand seeing you cry. I never could. But that night when the police showed up and said there'd been an accident . . . When I think about it, when I consider that we almost lost our little girl—" His voice cracked, and Trisha was jolted. She'd never seen her father get emotional this way. He got mad and yelled, but never teary.

"Daddy—"

He took a deep breath and regained his composure. "You have a future, Trisha. You have a lifetime of tomorrows. I want you to live every one of them."

"I do too. It's just so hard to think about all of them now. I'm so mixed up. I—I miss Christina so much." She began to cry softly.

"I know, baby. For a very long time you'll be dividing your life into two categories: before the accident and after the accident. The wreck is the line, the place where your childhood ended and adulthood began. I'd give anything if I could take you back to the other side of that line. But I can't. No one can."

"I know what you and Mom want for me, Dad. I once wanted it too. I don't know how to go forward. I feel stuck in the middle of a nightmare."

"You are stuck. But you'll find your way out, because you're smart and beautiful and wonderful."

She eyed him and offered a slight smile. "Says you."

"And I'm never wrong about such things."

He took her in his arms and held her. "How about we come up with a plan. We'll fill out the paperwork to secure your entrance into IU. Then at the end of the summer, we'll see how you're doing, and if you want to go, you'll be all set."

"And if I don't?"

"We won't make you, Trisha. We can't. This has to be something you want bad enough to go all out for. College isn't easy, so you've got to want it. You'll know a whole lot more about yourself in another six months. Trust me."

"I do, Daddy." She hugged him hard, holding on for dear life.

"Get out of the bathroom, Charlie—now! Don't make me late for school." Trisha pounded on the door of the bathroom she shared with her brother. By Monday, she'd forged a truce with her parents, with no one bringing up the subject of college. It would be one more thing for her to think about, but at least she didn't have to think about it anytime soon.

"I'm busy." Charlie yelled.

"Get *un*busy, and I mean right now." She rattled the doorknob.

"I locked it."

"Listen, you little dork-face, I'll get a ladder and come through the window if—"

The door flew open. Charlie stood wrapped in a towel, his hair slick with water. "What did you call me?"

"A dork-face." She leaned forward as if to threaten him.

He broke out in a smile.

"What's so funny? You look like a grinning fool."

"You called me a name."

"I have others for you."

"Don't you get it?" His grin was wider. "You're yelling at me again. You haven't yelled at me since the accident, and now you are."

She straightened. "And it makes you happy to have me yell at you?"

"Sure does. It means you're back!"

The power of his logic struck her profoundly. She *hadn't* been yelling at him. Wrapped in her own pain, she had been ignoring him. She thought back to the night she lay in the hospital and to his frightened little face and trembling voice. Despite her present irritation, she felt a smile creep across her mouth. "You're definitely a dork-face, so, yes, I guess I'm back."

"All right!" Charlie leaped up and gave her a high five. She slapped his hand, then grabbed his wrist and pulled him past her into the hall. "Hey!" he yelped.

She ran into the bathroom, slammed the door, and locked it. "I won't be long," she called out to him, laughing heartily about what Charlie considered a breakthrough.

When Trisha pulled up to Cody's house after school on Tuesday, Tucker Hanson's truck was parked in the driveway. Tucker's dad had bought him a small black pickup truck with a roll bar to replace the car that had been totaled in the accident. "It's supposed to be a whole lot safer," Tucker had told his friends. Trisha wondered what Christina would have thought of it, because they'd often made fun of guys in trucks.

"What do you call a guy with a pickup truck and a horn?" Christina would ask if guys in a truck passed them, honked, waved, and shouted for attention.

"Multitalented, because he can burp and say his name at the same time," Trisha would answer. And the two of them would break into peals of laughter and ignore the boys.

Trisha found Cody and Tucker in Cody's basement; in the background the TV replayed a football game. Cody held out his hand to her. "This is my girl," he announced, a look of pride on his face.

"Tucker knows that," she said.

"Cody and I were getting reacquainted," Tucker told her. "I brought him a tape of the Super Bowl we watched together in January."

"I don't remember watching it," Cody said. "But I remember football. That's good, don't you think?"

"I think it's in your DNA code," she said. Both boys grinned. She felt awkward, suddenly thinking that Christina should have been there.

"I came by to show Cody my new wheels."

"I like the truck. Your other car was black."

"Yes, a Pontiac."

Cody scrunched up his forehead. "With silver hubs. And mud flaps."

"Yes." Tucker glanced at Trisha.

"Well, don't I feel special," she said. "I'm a blank in his mind, but your mud flaps make the grade."

Cody blushed. "You're not really mad, are you? Some things come back in a flash, and I never know when that's going to happen."

She kissed his cheek. "I'm not mad. Just teasing."

"Was it hard for you to drive again?" Cody asked Tucker.

"The first time I sat behind the wheel after the wreck, my hands shook so bad I couldn't even turn on the ignition. I thought I was going to throw up."

"How about you?" Cody turned the question to Trisha.

"I'm all right about driving. At first I didn't think I would be able to, but I can. I'm driving my dad's old clunker now. He got a new one so that I could have a car." It had been generous of her parents to sacrifice so that she could get around. Christina had usually driven Trisha around. Now Trisha drove alone.

Tucker said, "My dad took me by the salvage yard to look at my car a few weeks ago. It's totaled. The roof was crushed, and there wasn't a piece of glass in it that wasn't broken. I couldn't believe any of us got out of it alive." Tucker's knuckles had gone white, gripping the arms of his chair as he described the car's condition.

One of us didn't, Trisha thought, but she knew he needed no reminding.

"I don't remember any of it," Cody said.

"Lucky you," Tucker said, his eyes full of pain.

"It's all like shadows to me," Cody said. "Sometimes I think I see something that looks familiar, but then it vanishes and I can't get hold of it again. The girl who died, Christina . . . I have her picture, but I don't know if she looks familiar because I remember her or because I've looked at her picture so much."

"She was beautiful," Tucker said. "I miss her more than anything in this world." Tucker struggled to his feet. Trisha could see that he was shaken. "I've got to go."

"Will you come back?" Cody asked.

"Do you want me to?"

"We were friends. I'm not sure I had that many."

"You did," Tucker said. "You were a regular guy. Everybody liked you."

His use of the past tense wasn't lost on Trisha.

At the foot of the stairs, Tucker said, "You two hold on to each other. Okay?"

Trisha watched him take the stairs two at a time, as if he were being chased by a ghost.

* * *

Trisha found a note from her mother stuck to the refrigerator door when she got home. It read: *I've taken Charlie to b'ball practice. Julia called. She would like to see you. They're moving.*

Sixteen

Trisha drove to Christina's house on Saturday morning in the rain. She hadn't been there since a week before the accident, which made her feel ashamed of herself. She'd known Christina's parents for as long as she'd known Christina, and she'd always liked them. She should have come by before now, before poor Julia had to call and ask her.

She pulled into the driveway. Julia stepped onto the porch, and Trisha realized that the woman must have been waiting and looking for her. Trisha hadn't seen her since the funeral and thought Julia looked thin, delicate, almost waiflike. "Hello," Christina's mom called, smiling as Trisha stepped out of her car.

Trisha, dodging raindrops, jogged up to the porch, where they stood looking at each other. "I—I'm sorry—" Trisha began.

"No apologies necessary." Julia waved her off. "Come into the kitchen. I made us hot chocolate."

Just entering the house felt dreamlike to Trisha. Every nook was as familiar to her as those in her own home. Yet things had changed too. Pictures had been removed from walls, and the living room looked uninhabited. In the kitchen, Julia made small talk as she set a plate of cookies on the table and poured steaming mugs of chocolate.

She invited Trisha to sit, saying, "It's good to see you. How have you been?"

"All right." Trisha cradled the mug, mostly to warm her freezing hands. She couldn't look Julia in the eye just yet. "Mom said you're moving."

"Yes. Nelson's company had an opening in Cleveland and offered him the position."

"When will you go?"

"They want us there by mid-April." Julia glanced around the kitchen. "Packing up is a real chore. Movers will do most of it. But, as always, there are things we must do."

Trisha nodded. "I remember moving from Chicago. It was hard."

"Right now, it's harder to stay. I'm glad we're going. Too many memories."

Trisha met her gaze. "I should have come by sooner."

"No. It's okay. I know how difficult this must be for you."

Julia's kindness touched her. "Mr. Eckloe . . . how is he?"

"Better than he was the night of the viewing." Julia pressed the bridge of her nose with her thumb and forefinger. "He must have seemed like a madman to everyone, especially Tucker."

"His reaction was understandable."

"We've talked to the police and have come to realize that it was an accident. It was just a senseless, stupid accident."

For a moment, neither of them spoke, and Trisha heard the rain hitting the kitchen window and saw it running down in rivulets, like tears. "I'll never forget her, you know," Trisha said.

"I know that. She loved you like a sister. She often said to me, 'Mom, if I ever had a sister, I'd want it to be Trisha.' "

A lump swelled in Trisha's throat.

"She loved Tucker too," Julia added. "I didn't always approve of the way he treated her, though."

Julia's announcement surprised Trisha. It must have shown, because Julia added, "I was sensitive to their relationship. I knew he sometimes made her unhappy."

"He didn't want her to go off to college."

"Selfish of him."

"That was his idea of love."

"You do think she would have gone whether he wanted her to or not, don't you?"

Trisha thought about her answer and saw no reason to mention the marriage offer Tucker had been planning to make. "Yes, I'm sure she would have gone. She knew what she wanted and wouldn't have let Tucker take it away from her."

Julia relaxed. "It's hard raising kids. We loved her so much and tried to do everything we could for her."

"She wanted you to be happy with her." Trisha knew how conflicted Christina had been about her feelings for Tucker and her desire to do what her parents wanted. Trisha thought of her own college dilemma and understood the gift her parents had given her by not applying pressure and trying to make her decide something she wasn't ready to decide.

"If you sit on a child too hard, they break. If you give them too much freedom, they don't learn limits," Julia said thoughtfully.

"You were great parents," Trisha said.

Sadness filled Julia's face. "The high school said they'd give us an honorary diploma for her. All her teachers said she was passing with As, but the rules say a child has to attend so many days before she can graduate. Stupid rule."

Trisha squirmed. Julia's sadness was breaking her heart.

Julia dabbed at her eyes with a napkin, then leaned forward, businesslike. "One of the reasons I wanted to see you is that before we dismantle Christina's room, I thought there might be some things in it you'd want. You know, to remember her by."

Trisha blanched. "Oh, I don't—"

"Please, come see. Make sure. She would want you to have anything she owned."

Reluctantly Trisha followed Julia upstairs and down the hallway toward Christina's room. She steeled herself as Julia opened the door for her. "Take your time," Julia said. "Take anything you want. I mean anything. I'll wait for you in the kitchen."

Julia was gone before Trisha could say a word. Trembling, she walked inside the room. It was like stepping through a time warp. The room was exactly as it had been the last time Trisha had seen it. Posters of a popular boy band graced the sunny yellow walls. The bed was made with the soft white coverlet that Trisha and Christina had bought when they were in the tenth grade. The bulletin board was crammed with photos, dried flowers, ticket stubs, the program from the time they'd gone to Chicago to see a Broadway-style play. Christina's dresser was lined with bottles of hair gels and hair sprays, pots of lip gloss, eye shadows, and hair baubles. Stuffed animals sat along the edges of a bookcase where Christina had last posed them. Half-burned candles and sticks of incense sat on a windowsill.

Trisha half expected Christina to burst into the room with a bowl full of popcorn and a couple of colas, their favorite after-school snack. She waited, but Christina didn't come, would never come again. Finally, Trisha began to walk around the room and touch Christina's things. In some ways, it was like touching her. Trisha expected it to freak her out, but it didn't. She found it comforting, almost soothing. Christina was still among her things. Her favorite fragrances laced the stale air like whispers, saying, *"I'm here. Right here."*

Trisha picked up a perfume bottle, spritzed it, and closed her eyes and breathed in her friend's essence. The scent of the lemon-lime concoction reminded Trisha of summer and lazy days at the pool—days that would never come again. She studied the images on the bulletin board, pictures from the past, of Christina and Tucker, Trisha and Christina, Trisha and Cody . . . Together they presented a story of a life half-lived, of a promise made but unkept. Life was gone for one of them. The others lingered on like half-finished portraits. Trisha, Cody, Tucker—they were the same but different now. So very, very different.

Trisha crossed to Christina's closet and opened the doors. The hangers were stuffed to capacity with Christina's clothes. Trisha fingered the tops, skirts, a row of pressed jeans, and even the cheerleader uniform. She recalled the day—it was at the end of their sophomore year—that Christina made the team.

"You won't hate me because now I'm one of them, will you?" Christina had asked.

At the time, Trisha had felt pangs of jealousy, of being left out of the tight little world that belonged to pretty, popular girls with perfect smiles and winning personalities. "No more than you hate me for being on the yearbook staff," she'd replied.

"You'll be the editor by the time you're a senior," Christina had said.

"No way."

"Way!" Christina had countered.

And of course, Christina's prediction had come true.

The uniform hung in the closet, discarded and useless. Their senior year, Christina had quit the squad right after football season ended. "More time with the books," she'd told Trisha.

More time with Tucker, Trisha had suspected. He'd never liked the way the guys ogled his girlfriend when she was on the squad.

Trisha was unaware of time passing, but realized it must've when she heard the grandfather clock downstairs chime one o'clock.

Knowing it was time to go, she glanced around quickly to fulfill the mission Julia had sent her on. She picked up the bottle of perfume, a flowered top she'd often borrowed when she'd wanted to feel "summery," a bracelet that sparkled with green and yellow crystals, and a romance novel they'd read together and loved when they were juniors.

Julia met her when she came down. "Is that all you want?"

"These are the things that remind me of her the most," Trisha said, still uncomfortable about taking anything at all.

"Then take them with our blessings. Here, I've got a bag for you." Julia held out a plastic grocery sack, and Trisha slipped her possessions inside.

"I should go. I told Mom I'd be back by lunch."

"Certainly. Of course." Julia didn't move. "May I ask a favor?"

"Anything."

"Would you let me hold you for just a minute?" Tears shimmered on Julia's lashes.

"Hold me? Well, gee, sure."

As Julia wrapped her arms around Trisha, Trisha felt the woman's body shudder. "It feels so good to hold a child in my arms again. Not that she let me cuddle her once she was a teenager. She was too big, too old . . . you know. But how I wanted to! When she was a child, she'd sit in my lap and I'd read to her, and sometimes the sunlight would bounce off her pretty golden curls. She used all those gels to straighten her pretty hair. She hated how curly it was."

Trisha shut her eyes, saw the images Julia painted, and felt her throat close tight.

"I miss her so much. So much."

"Me too," Trisha managed to say.

Julia pulled away, her face wet. "Thank you. Your parents are so lucky to have you. Kiss your mother for me."

"Will you write?"

"A Christmas card, I promise."

Trisha stepped onto the porch; Julia followed. The rain had stopped.

Julia said, "I put fresh flowers on her grave yesterday. I know they'll only die, but it made me feel better to visit her. She loved pretty flowers."

Trisha got into her car and drove away, left with the image of Julia forlorn but waving from the front porch, a memory she would never erase.

"Hello Mrs. Kimble. Remember me?"

The nurse looked up from behind the desk and broke into a smile. "Why, Trisha Thompson! How good to see you, girl." She came from around the desk and took Trisha's hands in hers. "My, my, you look so good. So much better than the last time I saw you. Your face is all healed and your crutches are gone." Her gaze swept Trisha head to toe. "Any lasting effects?"

None that show, Trisha almost said. "No. I'm recovered from the accident."

"So what brings you here to the nursing home? Anything I can do for you?"

"Actually, I was hoping I could do something for you."

"And what's that?"

"I've been thinking about Christina's old volunteering job. I was wondering if it was filled. If maybe I could have it."

Seventeen

Mrs. Kimble looked surprised. "Well, goodness, girl, I'll never refuse good, free help. But what about school? Shouldn't you be doing fun things?"

"Don't you know about the senior blahs? All I want is to get out of there." More and more Trisha had turned the yearbook project over to Frank. She simply didn't have the interest for it anymore. School felt like a prison, her classes like solitary confinement.

"You sure you want to work here?"

"Real sure. I know it gave Christina a lot of satisfaction. So, is a job available?"

"Of course it's available. There's a volunteer schedule posted on the bulletin board. All you have to do is sign up and sign in when you arrive. If you can't come, call us so that we can shift things around."

"Sounds simple. When can I start?"

"Tuesday. That's when the new schedule is out."

Trisha nodded, anxious but satisfied. "I—I probably won't be as good at the job as . . . my friend, but I'll try very hard not to let you down."

Mrs. Kimble tipped her head, her brown eyes thoughtful. "It takes a long time to fill up a hole in your heart, Trisha. If this will help, then go for it. If you change your mind, you just come tell me. I'll understand."

"Thanks, but I won't change my mind. Christina always liked you," Trisha added.

"And I always admired and liked her. What happened was a real pity. Lordy, yes, a real pity."

Trisha's parents weren't too pleased with her decision, but to their credit, they didn't give her any arguments. Cody was very understanding. "If it's what you want to do, then you should do it," he said when she told him following school on Monday.

"I'll still be coming to see you, so don't think you can slack off and stop being my boyfriend," she told him.

"You still want me for a boyfriend?"

"Naturally. Why wouldn't I?"

"It just seems like a girl as pretty as you could have any guy she wanted. Instead you pick a lame-brain like me."

"Don't you ever call yourself names, you hear?" She shook her finger under his nose. "You're not a 'lame-brain.' You're my boyfriend, and I won't have anybody running you down. Not even *you*."

"It's just so hard sometimes, Trisha. I think I'm getting better, then without warning, my mind goes completely blank. I can't think of a simple word or how to solve a math problem. My homeschool teacher is really understanding, but I know that I'm different now than I was before the accident. I'll never catch up."

His pessimism cut through her heart. The accident had wrecked so many things. "All you can do is try," she said.

"I am trying. That's what's so bad. No matter how hard I try, sometimes it doesn't make a difference. I want to graduate with our class.

I want to think about the future, but it's just too hard for me to make any plans."

"Stuck in neutral," she said. "That's what I call it. We can't go back. We can't go forward. We're just plain stuck."

"Maybe I should have stayed in the coma. It would have been easier on everybody."

"Don't say that. It was horrible for everyone—for you of course, as well as for your family. I wanted to talk to you, but I couldn't. At least now we can be together."

"When I woke up in the hospital, I felt like I was floating out of a fog and landing on a bed like a feather. I didn't know who I was. My mom looked familiar, but I couldn't remember who she was. Can you imagine not recognizing your own mother?"

"But that didn't last long."

"Yes . . . but I want everything the way it was before. It's been more than two months since the accident, and I still can't return to school."

"You will, but believe me, it's pretty boring at school. Personally, I can't wait until the year's over."

"Then what?"

"I don't know, Cody," she answered honestly. "That's still the big question in my mind too."

"You should move on. You don't need me in your life complicating things."

Trisha took his hand in hers, studied his fingers, remembered the way he used to touch her before the accident. "Don't you see? We've been through something together that no one else can ever understand the way we do. Who's going to be patient with me when I'm in a crowd and a sudden memory hits and I start crying? I have no history with anyone but you. I can't think about dating another guy, hoping he'll be understanding without me having to explain every time I fall apart."

"But that's just the point, Trisha. I don't remember. And it's making me crazy."

"You don't remember now," she said. "But you will. I know you will."

"Come to Florida with us," Abby begged Trisha as spring break approached. "We'll have fun and get tans and play volleyball on the beach and pester Frank and all his friends."

"Not interested," Trisha said. "Cody's here. Besides, I'm making progress with Mr. Tappin."

When Abby looked blank, Trisha added, "He's an old man with Alzheimer's who lives at the home. Sort of a special project of mine. He won't eat unless somebody feeds him and even then, he won't eat for just anybody. But if I feed him, he eats."

Abby made a face. "Gee, the excitement must be overwhelming for you."

"Don't be mean. He was a special project of Christina's too. He has no one, you know. He's all alone."

"Does the old guy yell? My neighbor's mother got Alzheimer's and she swore worse than any HBO comedian."

"He doesn't speak at all. He doesn't even leave his room unless we put him in a wheelchair and take him outside. He's totally withdrawn."

"Ugh! What a life. It's nice of you to care about him, though. Sorry if I came off as insensitive."

"I used to feel the same way whenever I went to the home to help Christina. Now I don't think anything about it at all. And I feel better doing something that's helping somebody else."

Abby looked pensive. "So is that what

you're going to do? Fill in the blanks that Christina left behind?"

Trisha bristled. "That's not fair. I'm doing a good thing here. And I'm doing it because I want to."

"Hey, hey . . . I don't mean to offend you. Sure, you're doing a nice thing. I'm only asking you *why* you're doing it."

"Because I want to. Because I don't want to go through my whole life and feel like I never made some kind of difference in the world."

"You're not that old," Abby pointed out. "You've got plenty of time to impact the world."

"You think so? I once thought so too, but now I don't. We all thought Christina had plenty of time. But we were wrong, weren't we? In truth, how much time do any of us really have?"

After her friends left town for spring break, Trisha busied herself with working at the nursing home, visiting Cody, and helping her mother with several spring-cleaning projects around the house. She missed her friends, and felt restless and unfocused no matter how active she strived to be. She even filled out a job application at Home Depot, but her parents had a fit and forbade her to turn it in.

In the middle of the week, while her mother took Charlie to the dentist, Trisha was puttering around the house when the doorbell rang. She found Tucker on her porch. "Can I come in?" he asked.

Seeing him dressed in a suit, she almost asked, *"Who died?"* because she hadn't seen him in a suit since Christina's funeral. She decided the question was in bad taste. "You want a soda?" She led him to the kitchen, burning with curiosity as to why he'd come. She'd known he wasn't going away for spring break, but she hadn't expected to see him until classes resumed.

"No thanks," he said, sitting at the table and removing his sunglasses. His eyes were red-rimmed. When he spoke again, he said, "It's over."

"What's over?"

"The coroner's inquest. I went before a judge yesterday and then again today to tell my story, then he ruled on the accident."

Trisha went hot and cold all over. For some reason, she thought she'd have known about the hearing in advance, but now it was all over. The news was upsetting. "And . . . ?"

"The accident's been ruled an accident, not vehicular homicide." He sagged in the chair. "I wasn't blamed."

She turned his words over in her mind, not sure how to respond or even how to feel about the verdict.

"There were a lot of factors about that night that contributed," Tucker said. "The ice, the other car, the flap at the game. But speed wasn't one of them. I wasn't speeding, so the judge ruled that I wasn't at fault."

She had an instantaneous image of his hand on the gearshift and of Cody saying *"Slow down."* "Okay," she said, her voice feeling stuck in the back of her throat. "I guess that settles it then."

"I came here first to tell you because I thought you should hear it from me."

"What about Christina's parents?"

"They were notified about the hearing, but they didn't show. I talked to them just before they moved, though. I wanted them to know how sorry I was about . . . everything. Her father said he was sorry about how he treated me at the funeral home. I told him I understood.

He said that nothing would bring Christina back, that making me suffer wouldn't change anything."

Trisha tried to digest all that Tucker had said. She'd known the Eckloes for years, and now they were gone. Christina was gone. Cody was deeply wounded. Tucker had been judged blameless at the hearing. Nobody was to blame. It had been happenstance, fate, a fluke, bad timing. All was forgiven.

"Are you going to be all right?" Tucker asked. "You look really pale."

"Was your lawyer with you at the hearing?"

"Yes. He was representing me."

"But you told your story to the judge?"

"Yes."

"And now it's over?"

Tucker hunched forward, rested his fore-arms against his knees, and stared down at the floor. "It'll never be over, will it? The only girl I ever loved is dead, and I was driving the car when she died. That's the bottom line, isn't it?"

She didn't agree but knew it was the truth. "I know your parents are glad you're not being blamed," she said.

"Yes, they've supported me all the way." He stood. "Will you tell Cody?" he asked.

She said she would and watched him make his way toward the front door. She braced her arms on the countertop and listened while his car pulled out of the driveway and drove away. She stood staring out the window over the sink where a vine in an old clay pot was trying to send out new shoots of green. The ordeal was over. Tucker was blameless in the eyes of the law. Christina had died in an accident. And yet, ever since the night of the crash, a memory she couldn't grab hold of kept haunting her. And now, even if she did remember, what possible good would it do?

Eighteen

———— ✂ ————

Cody's family and doctors allowed him to return to school following spring break. As Trisha walked proudly at his side, kids greeted him in the halls like a long-lost voyager.

"I feel like a freak," he admitted when they were standing at his locker before the first bell sounded.

"Why? Everyone's knocked out that you're back. This is what you said you wanted, isn't it—to be back?"

"Sure, I want to be here. It's just that Mom's arranged with my teachers for me to have special treatment."

"Such as?"

"Stupid stuff. I get extra time to get to classes. If I want to leave before a class is over, I can get up, walk out, and go to the office and wait for the next class to start. In short, I don't have to play by regular rules."

"And you think you've got a problem? A lot of us would love your problem."

"Don't you get it? It tells people that I'm 'different,' that poor Cody can't cut it and needs special handling. I don't want special privileges."

Actually, Trisha thought special treatment was a good idea. Cody's attention span was still brief, and he had trouble with self-control when he became frustrated. "Do you know what stuff you want from your locker?" she asked, changing the subject.

He didn't answer but stood staring at his locker door.

"What's wrong?" Trisha asked.

"I can't open it."

She followed his gaze to the lock and realized what he meant. "I know your combination," she said quickly. "Want me to open it?"

"Yes, open it." He sounded upset.

She shielded her hands from passersby and

quickly spun the combination. When the locker was open, she said, "You can get a key lock and change it to a new combination."

"No," he said. "Please write down the combination for me. I'll use my time in study hall to memorize it. It'll be something to do so that I don't walk out," he added sarcastically.

Her heart went out to him. "It'll get better, Cody."

"When?" he asked.

She had no answer for him.

When word swept through the school that Tucker had been acquitted of any wrongdoing in the accident, people stopped talking about their spring breaks and started talking about him. Trisha found it hard to hear the whole incident rehashed everywhere she turned. She didn't hide her feelings either. When she walked into the bathroom and overheard two junior girls gossiping about it, she glared at them and said, "Don't you two have anything better to talk about?"

One said, "Gee, we didn't mean anything by it."

"Then shut up about it."

"It's a free country," one girl dared to say.

"Then I might just take advantage of my freedom to stick your head down a toilet."

The girl's eyes widened. "No need to go postal about it. We were just talking."

The other girl took her friend's arm. "Let's get out of here."

Trisha let them pass, still angry but knowing she had overreacted. People were going to gossip. She hated it but couldn't change it.

"It'll blow over," Abby said later when Trisha told her what had happened.

"But why do they have to talk about it at all? Some of them hardly knew Christina. It's disrespectful."

"It was a big event, Trisha. Nobody expects to lose someone who's only seventeen, someone you see every day in the halls and in your classrooms."

"She wasn't 'lost.' She died."

"Trisha, I've got to say this to you. It sounds like your problem's with Tucker. Like you're mad because he didn't get charged with the accident."

Hot tears stung Trisha's eyes. "She was my *best friend*, Abby. Best friends don't grow on trees, you know."

"I know. I've told you, I know. Neither do brothers," Abby said.

Later that same week, when Trisha used a hall pass to go to the girls' room, she saw Cody sitting on a bench in the commons. He was staring at a card that listed his courses and the room numbers of his classrooms. "What's up?" she asked, peering over his shoulder.

"I got lost. I can't find my way to government class."

Pity for him washed over her. "It happens. The school's so darn big."

"I feel stupid."

"Please don't."

He turned to her, his blue eyes filled with pain. "Can you show me the way? I'm already really late and everybody stares when I come in late."

"Want to sit it out?" she asked.

"I can't. I'm already so far behind."

She realized that in spite of his mother's and the school's best efforts, all the bases hadn't been covered. "Follow me," she said, silently vowing that he would never suffer this indignity again if she could help it.

She formulated a plan to help him. Because

his doctor had yet to clear him to drive, his mother dropped him off in the morning, and Trisha drove him home after school. To make sure he was covered during school hours, Trisha enlisted Frank and Abby to help shadow Cody until they were all sure he could manage on his own. She never told him because she didn't want to embarrass him, and by the end of April, her efforts had paid off. Cody had completely relearned the layout of the school and could sit in class for the full fifty minutes. He still struggled through tests, and his memory returned in snippets and fragments, never fully formed, but Trisha considered it progress. Cody needed even small successes to feel whole again.

"We are going to prom together, aren't we?" Cody asked Trisha one afternoon as they stood in the commons, checking out a poster announcing the upcoming dance.

"Do you want to go? It really doesn't mean that much to me."

"It's prom. We should go. I've talked to Frank, who said we can double with him and Abby."

"If we go with anybody, they'd be my

choice," Trisha said. They both left unsaid what they were thinking: if the accident hadn't happened, they would have automatically gone with Christina and Tucker.

"Did I used to like wearing rented tuxedos?" he asked.

"You said a tux made you feel like a penguin without an ice floe."

"Wasn't I the funny guy. How do you feel about me in a tux?"

"I like you in one," she admitted. "Makes you look rich and famous."

"Then it's settled. I'm wearing one just for you." Cody wrapped his arm around her waist. "Sometimes not being able to remember everything about the past isn't such a bad thing, is it? It means I can be retrained. Like a puppy."

She giggled. "That's funny."

"You think so? Hey, I made a joke, didn't I?" His face broke into a grin. "So does this mean we're in 'puppy love'?"

She laughed again, pleased to see him so happy with himself. For the first time in months, she saw signs of the old Cody shining through. "Either that or puppy poo," she answered.

"You're talking dirty, girl. Tell me more."

They poked fun at each other and laughed all the way to the parking lot.

On Saturday, Trisha and Abby rode the train into Chicago to search for the perfect prom dresses. They walked in the bright spring sunshine up Michigan Avenue past the *Chicago Tribune* building, crossed over the river, and headed toward Marshall Field's.

"You ever shop Filene's?" Abby asked. "It has great prices, and I haven't got that much to spend. Maybe we should start there."

Trisha started to say, *"But Field's is Christina's favorite, so we always go there first,"* but she stopped herself. Things were different now. Abby was turning into a good friend, and Christina was no longer around for Trisha to follow. Trisha said, "Sounds like a good place to begin."

"I mean, if you'd rather go to Field's—"

"No. Filene's is fine. I don't have much money to spend either." As she said it, Trisha felt as if a weight were lifting off her heart.

The girls crossed the avenue and headed away from the river.

Just before prom night, Trisha's and Cody's parents offered to pay for a limo and driver to usher the two couples around for the night. "Some kids rent limos, but it's not for us," Trisha told her father. "But thanks anyway."

"Hey, you'll look like VIPs," he said. "Or movie stars. These things come with refrigerators and food and sodas—sort of a living room on wheels. Come on—live a little."

And leave the driving to someone else, was what he was really saying, she realized.

"We'll be okay, Daddy. Frank's a good driver and we're not going to any all-night parties after the dance. Cody's mom won't let him." Cody had been mad about that part, but Trisha had insisted she didn't want to stay out all night anyway.

He father looked self-conscious. "All right, you caught me. Your mom and I want you to have fun, but we also want you to be safe." She opened her mouth to protest, but he cut her off. "I know, I know. Frank is great. We don't care. Besides, it's not only about safety. It's also something we want to do for you kids because we love you. Don't be insulted. And don't give us a hard time. Just take the limo."

Trisha sighed. "Just don't pick one that's over-the-top," she said.

On prom night, Cody's mother brought

him to Trisha's house, where a long, white, and embarrassingly garish limousine waited in the driveway. Everything on the car was white, inside and out. It even had white faux-fur pillows in the seat corners and fuzzy white floor mats. When it first pulled up, Trisha wailed, "Daddy! What were you thinking?"

"It was all that was available. Everyone rented before we did," her father said with a shrug. "Besides, you can't miss it in a crowd."

But Cody pronounced it cool, and Charlie crawled around the backseats, inspecting doors, knobs, compartments, refrigerator contents, the console television set, and video selections. Trisha's parents stood on the porch, camera in hand, while the driver opened the door for Trisha and Cody. "You both look beautiful," her mother called.

Charlie made a gagging sound and flopped against the porch rail.

The driver picked up Abby and Frank at Abby's house and, after another round of picture taking, drove the thirty-minute stretch to the country club where the dance was being held. Cars jammed the parking lot, a line of limos queued in the circular driveway. Light spilled onto a column of stone steps where a throng of seniors dressed in dark tuxes and shimmery gowns filed into the elegant lobby, heading toward the grand ballroom.

As the limo waited in line, Trisha eased down the window and surveyed the field of chauffeured black automobiles. "Cody, we have the only hundred-foot white one here. This is *so* embarrassing."

Abby got the giggles.

"What's your point?" Frank asked.

"Am I the only one embarrassed by this?" Trisha asked, trying to sound huffy but losing the battle. It had become very funny to her too.

"I'm not embarrassed," Cody said, flipping a furry pillow in the air. "Are you embarrassed, Frank?"

"No way. I think of it as preparation for future stardom." He batted the pillow away.

Abby kept giggling. "My mascara's running."

"Well, go catch it," Cody told her.

They all heaved with laughter. Even when the driver pulled in front of the steps and opened the door for them, they couldn't exit the car right away because they were laughing so hard. Finally Trisha scooted out, took Cody's hand, and started up the steps. At the top she turned and came face to face with

Tucker Hanson. He was dressed in a tuxedo and standing by himself, completely and utterly alone. Trisha had heard that he hadn't asked anyone to prom. She saw now that it was true.

As his gaze bore into hers, it was as if a bolt of lightning shot through her. Her laughter died in her throat, and cold, ghostly fingers gripped her heart. Tucker's eyes held a recriminating message: *How can you be having a good time? How can you forget her?*

Oblivious to the drama happening between Trisha and Tucker, Cody said, "Hey, Tuck."

"Hello," he answered.

"You want to hang with us tonight?" Frank asked.

"No," he said, catching Trisha's eye. "I won't be staying long."

Abby leaned forward and said into Trisha's ear, "Don't let this sour the evening for you. He's got no right to make you feel bad. You're allowed to have a good time."

Trisha nodded, but she wanted to ask, *How can I, with my best friend lying in her grave?*

But it wasn't until after the dance, when they had returned to the car, that the past really caught up with Trisha. She had just settled into the seat with Cody beside her and was looking out the window when another car slid past her line of sight. As she watched the faces in the other car pass by her, the fragmented pictures from the night of the accident fell perfectly into place. Trisha sat bolt upright. Suddenly, she knew what had happened the night of the accident.

She knew. She clearly remembered every detail.

Nineteen

———— ❧ ————

Trisha took her time deciding what to do about the memory that had returned to her on prom night. She turned the details over and over, making sure she remembered everything correctly. She told no one else, not even Cody, what she now knew to be true. And days later, once she had everything locked in her mind, she went looking for Tucker Hanson.

She found him sitting with a group of his friends in the cafeteria. With her heart thudding, she walked over and announced, "We need to talk."

He looked up. "Well, sure, Trisha. Do you need another picture of me for the yearbook?"

His friends laughed at his joke, but she ignored them. "It's about Christina."

His cocky smile vanished. "What about Christina?"

"I'll tell you when I see you. I get off from work at the nursing home at five. Come there to meet me."

As she walked off, she heard one of Tucker's friends ask, "What was *that* all about?" *Let them wonder,* she thought. *Let Tucker explain his way out of this one.*

At the home, Trisha fed Mr. Tappin early, making sure he ate all his supper, all the while thinking about her upcoming confrontation. It had been a long time coming, but now that she knew the truth, she was going to make certain it got out in the open. She nursed cold, hard anger but vowed that once this was over, she would let Christina rest in peace.

Trisha signed out at five and found Tucker waiting for her in the parking lot, his black truck parked next to her car. He got out of his truck as she approached. "You ready to tell me what this is about?" His tone was casual, but his eyes were wary.

"I remembered something about the night of the accident."

"What?"

"Not here," she said.

"Then where?"

"You know where," she said, slamming the door.

He didn't say a word but got into the truck and put it into gear. He waited while she went to her car and got in. They both knew where they were going.

As she approached the site of the accident, Trisha felt her mouth go dry and her hands grow cold. Tucker parked on the shoulder of the road at the same place where his car had slid and careened into the field and overturned. She pulled in behind his truck. May sunlight spilled over the landscape like warm honey. Trees sprouted green leaves, spring wildflowers bloomed along the roadside, and in the field, heavy black dirt that had been freshly turned waited to be planted with rows of corn.

Trisha slid out of her car and stood gazing out over the field, an aching sadness pressing against her heart. No visible damage remained from the accident; the earth looked whole and new again.

Tucker came around to stand beside her, his arms folded across his chest. "Can we talk now?"

Without looking at him, she said, "You passed on the right side. You couldn't get around the other car on the left because it kept speeding up, trapping you behind it. So you put your car into a lower gear and tried to shoot around them to the right, on the shoulder of the road. That's why you hit the ice. That's why you lost control."

"Is that what you remember?"

"When the police talked to me, I told them that the roads were clear that night, freshly salted. So in order for you to have hit ice and lost control, you had to be on the shoulder, where it hadn't been salted." She rested her back on the truck's fender, which was still warm from the spinning of the tires. "What I didn't remember before, but do now, is glancing out my window and seeing the boys' faces in the other car as we passed them. They looked shocked because they hadn't expected you to do that—to pass on the right. I wouldn't have remembered seeing their faces if you'd passed on the left, the way you're supposed to. It would have been impossible, because if you'd pulled around them on the left, their car would have been on Cody's side of the car, not mine."

She turned and faced him. "Did you really think you could get away with it? Were you counting on me having a permanent mental block about it?"

"No," he said. "I figured either you or Cody would remember eventually."

"Well, Cody isn't any threat, is he? I mean, the accident—*your* accident," she added hotly, "wiped his mind clean. That must have been a real plus for you."

"Stop it," Tucker said. "I never wanted that to happen to Cody. I never wanted any of it to happen."

"How could you have gone through the inquest and not told the truth?"

"I told the truth," he said, catching her off guard. "The police knew the truth because I told them. So did the guys in the other car. I wasn't speeding, but yes, I did pass illegally."

She didn't know whether or not to believe him. "And the judge still ruled that you weren't to blame?"

"Because Christina grabbed my arm," he said, his voice shaking. "She snatched my hand off the steering wheel and . . . and . . . I lost control of the car."

"You're blaming *Christina*?" Trisha was incredulous.

"No," he said quickly. "I'm blaming myself. I've always blamed myself. But she did grab my arm. It's no excuse, because I was trying to get around the other car on the right and I shouldn't have done that. The accident was my fault. My fault," he repeated. "I killed Christina."

Hearing him say the words was not nearly as satisfying as Trisha had imagined it would be. The sure knowledge hurt unbearably. As if he'd taken a knife and cut her heart open. She couldn't stop the hot tears that stung and burned her eyes. "And the judge *knew*? Her parents *knew*? And they let you walk away from it?"

"It wasn't a secret," he said. "I kept trying to pass the other car on the left—three, four, five times. Finally, the driver put the car in the center of the road, sort of like he was daring me to get past. I knew he wouldn't expect me to go to his right. I know I shouldn't have, but I did anyway. I would have made it too, except that when the tires crunched on the gravel on the shoulder, Christina panicked and grabbed the wheel. She turned it just enough. Then we hit ice and went airborne."

As he talked, the memories tumbled and fell on Trisha like lead pellets. She saw the boys' startled faces going by her window. She saw Tucker's hand on the gearshift, saw Christina's arm dart across the console to the steering wheel, and heard her scream, *"No! Don't!"* It was true. Everything Tucker said was true.

"And you were never going to tell anybody what really happened?"

"I wouldn't have denied it if it came out, but I wasn't going to go out of my way to spread it around either. 'Hey, look at me, everybody—I killed my girlfriend because I made a stupid mistake.' "

"You kept quiet to save face," she said bitterly. "You're a coward."

The muscles in his jaw worked, as if he were clenching his teeth. "Probably so. But you weren't the only one who lost someone they loved that night, Trisha. You've been acting like you're the only one who's hurting. I lost the only girl I ever loved. And I have no one to blame except myself."

"And by not telling the truth, everyone feels

sorry for you. 'Poor Tucker,' " she spit out the
words. "I *know* others are hurt. Her parents are
ruined forever!"

"Her parents said that ruining my life with a
lawsuit wouldn't bring her back," Tucker said,
ignoring Trisha's outburst. "I blubbered like a
baby, telling them I was sorry. They said they
forgave me, but I don't know how they can."

"And Cody's life too!" she cried. "Look at all
he's lost. He's not even the same person he
was before the accident."

"You can't say anything to me I haven't already said to myself. Will it make you feel better if I stand up in front of the whole school
and say, 'I killed Christina'? Is that what you
want?"

She didn't know what she wanted. She hurt
so badly at the moment that she couldn't
think straight. "You used to bully her, try to
force her to do what you wanted her to do.
You were never very nice to her, Tucker. You
tell me you loved her, but I know how much
you made her cry."

"I know that too." His eyes looked watery.
"I'd give anything if I could see her again. If I
could touch her and tell her how sorry I
am . . . about . . . everything."

"You can't turn back time," Trisha said. "No one can." It was too late for Tucker. And yet she knew Christina really loved him despite all his bad behavior. Her hate for him began to crumble. The burden of his guilt weighed far more than the pain of Trisha's loss. His knowledge of all that he'd done before and after Christina died was a permanent scar on his life.

Trisha walked away, but only got as far as the white-cross memorial. The cheerleading squad had kept its promise to maintain the memorial with flowers. A planter box had been erected around the base of the cross, and colorful pansies fluttered in the breezy twilight. She saw that someone had carved the initials CE and the date Christina had died in the center of the cross.

Trisha dropped to her knees in front of the box. She fingered the petals of the pansies, then buried her face in her hands and wept.

She felt Tucker's presence as he crouched beside her. "I'm sorry, Christina," he whispered. "So . . . sorry." He touched Trisha's shoulder. "Come on. Follow me back to town. Tomorrow you can tell people whatever you want. I don't care anymore."

* * *

Trisha went over to Cody's that night and told him what had happened with Tucker. He shook his head. "I don't remember any of it. It's all a blank. But I feel sorry for Tucker, because he can't ever get away from the memory. It'll be his curse for as long as he lives."

She told her parents too, and they were sorry but philosophical about it. "Maybe Tucker wasn't trying to hide the truth," Trisha's dad said. "He was probably just trying to get out from under the burden of it for a while. Knowing he caused someone to die and two others to be hurt so badly must have been a heavy load to carry."

"So you're telling me that you're not mad at him?"

"I'm furious with him." Her dad stroked her hair. "If it had been you who died, I'd probably have taken him apart with my bare hands. But I understand how Christina's parents feel too. Ruining Tucker's life by insisting that he go to jail for a lapse in judgment won't change a thing. It won't bring Christina back. And she did grab the steering wheel—not that I'm blaming her. Who knows what might have happened if she hadn't done that?"

In the end, Trisha didn't tell anyone at school. She was surprised, however, when Tucker did. He told one of his closer friends, who told another, who told another. The story spread through school, but not like malicious wildfire. It went from group to group to group like water seeping beneath a dam, touching everyone. Tucker's revelation changed nothing at school, since most kids felt sorry for him. Others considered it ancient history and said it should be put in the past—that the future was what mattered. Trisha had thought that having everybody know the truth about Tucker's real role in the accident would make her feel different, maybe even better. But it didn't.

Two weeks before graduation, Cody called Trisha to say, "It's official—I'm not going to graduate with our class."

Twenty

❧

Trisha couldn't believe Cody's bad news. "That's not fair! You've worked so hard! How can they do this to you?"

"I had too much stuff to relearn. I couldn't keep up with the new material. I'm at least half a year behind. And I missed too many days to qualify for passing." He sounded dejected.

"You should go before the school board. Your mom can persuade them to make an exception. None of this was your fault."

"I think my parents are relieved. They hate having me out of their sight—especially Mom. So now I have to stick around instead of going off to college. Remember how we were going to go to IU together? It's not going to happen."

"Well, that settles it. If you're staying here, so am I. I wasn't crazy about leaving in September anyway. I filled out the forms because my parents begged me to, but I don't have to go away if I don't want to."

"But what about college? You should go. You're smart and you've planned for years on going to college."

"I'll go to the community college," she said. "And I'll live at home and see you every day until you earn your diploma."

"You'd do that for me?"

"You bet I will. No matter what my parents say, I know this is what I want."

The graduation ceremony was held at the civic center at the end of the first week of June. Trisha put on the bright yellow robe and smiled for her parents' camera, but a part of her felt detached. It wasn't the senior year she'd planned or dreamed about. For years, she'd planned to make the walk with Christina and Cody. Yet now she was making it alone. Christina was gone and Cody was sitting in the audience with Trisha's family.

At the ceremony, the administration paid tribute to Christina's brief life by placing a blowup of the two-page memorial from the yearbook and a folded cap and gown on a chair onstage. Every senior who walked across the stage to receive a diploma passed the memorial. Many tossed mementos—flowers, school pennants, pom-poms, varsity letters— every kind of small token. Trisha passed the chair with tears in her eyes, pausing long enough to kiss the tips of her fingers and touch the mortarboard. "Goodbye, Christina," she whispered.

With summer upon her, Trisha found a job as a cashier in a store not far from her home and continued working at the nursing home in her off hours. She dated Cody and saw Abby whenever she could. When she heard the news that Tucker had gone to live with relatives in another state, she felt a deep relief. It helped to know she wouldn't see him around.

One night in July, Trisha's mother shook her awake. "What's wrong?" Trisha squinted from the glare of the bedside lamp. Her digital clock read 1:35 A.M.

"The nursing home called," her mother said. "They asked me to wake you to let you know that Mr. Tappin is dying."

Trisha hurried to the home, hoping and praying that the old man would hold on until she arrived. When she got there, she found Mrs. Kimble sitting by Mr. Tappin's bed reading a book.

"How is he?" Trisha asked.

"His breathing is labored," Mrs. Kimble said. "It won't be long now."

Trisha collapsed into a chair. "I'm so glad I made it in time."

"You didn't have to come, child."

"Yes, I did. You see, I promised him I wouldn't let him die alone." As she said the words, she realized how dumb they must sound. Mr. Tappin had Alzheimer's—he knew little of the world of reality.

Mrs. Kimble put her book aside. "I'll go down the hall to check on Mrs. Anderson while you wait."

When Trisha was alone, she picked up Mr. Tappin's hand. His skin felt dry and flaky. In the dim light from the wall lamp, he looked very old. His skin was pulled tight across his face, his eyes sunken in their sockets. His mouth was open, and his breath came in spurts with long stretches of silence in between. Trisha wanted to cry for him, but she couldn't. Death would free him from the prison of his diseased mind. Death would release his frail body from the shackles of age. His soul would be free to rise to heaven and wrap around eternity. She couldn't feel sorry for him. "Say hello to Christina when you see her," she said to him.

He lived another two hours. When his last breath came, Trisha squeezed his hand and laid it gently on the covers. She walked to the nurses' station, told Mrs. Kimble, and waited while another nurse went in to pronounce Mr. Tappin dead and to prepare his body for the funeral home. "How are you, my dear girl?" Mrs. Kimble asked.

"I'm not as sad as I thought I'd be," Trisha confessed. "I'm glad he's not suffering any longer. He's free now."

"You're free too, Trisha."

"What do you mean?"

"I don't want to see you around this place, as much as we love your help."

"But why?" Trisha hadn't expected Mr. Tappin's death to end her involvement with the nursing home.

"Because Mr. Tappin was the last tie you had to your friend Christina. It's over now. You can stop feeling bad that you're alive and she isn't."

Trisha flinched. "Is that what I've been doing?"

"Oh, dear girl . . . you been wishing for months that this old world would stop turning and let you get off. It's been plain as day. But tonight a chapter has closed. Tonight you are free to go on living."

Tears filled Trisha's eyes as she grasped what Mrs. Kimble was telling her. With Mr. Tappin's death, so many parts of her life with Christina were over. "I miss her so much."

"Ain't no shame in missing her. Ain't no shame in living without her. She's gone. You're here. Those are the facts." Mrs. Kimble leaned across the desk and took both of Trisha's hands in hers. A smile split her wide face. "Besides, there's something waiting on the side porch for you."

"What's that?"

"Your future."

Trisha discovered Cody sitting in the dark in a rocker on the east-facing porch. "What are you doing here?" She couldn't hide how glad she was to see him.

"Your mother called mine and told us about Mr. Tappin. I'm glad your mother isn't upset that you're sticking by me. I thought I should come and take you home when it was all over and she agreed. I didn't want you to be by yourself."

His thoughtfulness almost made her cry. "Thank you."

He pulled her into his lap. "You all right?"

"I'm all right. Since Mr. Tappin was so old and so sick, it wasn't as hard to face this death. I think he's with Christina in heaven now."

"While I've been sitting here, I've been doing some thinking. A lot of thinking, really."

"About what?"

"About how you stuck by me this year. About how you helped me make a comeback. I couldn't have done any of it without you. My parents, of course, are the greatest, but you— you made me want to hurry up and heal."

She laid her cheek against his shoulder. "I love you, Cody."

He kissed her temple. "And I love you. I may not remember many things from before the accident. I may never remember all of my life from before. Truth is, I don't even try to re-member it all anymore. I'm just taking it day by day. And the best part about every day is finding you in it."

Goose bumps raced up her arms, and her heart filled to overflowing. "Well, get used to it. I plan to be around for a long, long time."

"Forever?" he asked.

"Forever," she answered.

They sat curled in each other's arms and watched dawn spread rosy fingers through low, gray clouds and the sun slip over the hori-zon to begin a new day.